The
Ball
Of
Wisdom

Zephram Tino

Illustrated by Crystal Musseau

Tellwell Talent
www.tellwell.ca

ISBN
978-0-2288-2707-8 (Hardcover)
978-0-2288-2705-4 (Paperback)
978-0-2288-2706-1 (eBook)

Dedication

This book is dedicated to children who are currently or have ever been in the foster care system, and to those families who wrongfully lost their children to suicide while in government care.

Our one hope for this book is that it brought a
smile to that wonderful face of yours.
If you are a child, teen, or adult, there's a little
something in this story for you to enjoy.
Like my good friend Pirate Pete would say,
"Well, what works for the little matees, works
for grown up buccaneers too."

Sincerely,
The two eccentric teenagers who wrote, and illustrated this book
Zephram Tino
Crystal Musseau

Contents

Part One.. 1

Part Two 7

Part Three 21

Part Four 33

Margaret and Joan's Moderately Neato Adventure........................48

Part Five 64

Part Six..72

Epilogue 97

Acknowledgments 107

The Writer And The Illustrator 111

Jim Rimmer & The Alexander Quill Font 115

Part One

The Medieval times, a strange and different time. Where the woman's place was in the household, or locked in a ridiculously tall tower, in which they would await their knight in shining armour to be married off to a wealthy Prince (Arranged marriages were strange back then). However, one girl was going to turn this system on its keester. It all started in a kingdom, nestled between two mountains.

King Alloicious, the ruler of the kingdom sat before his knights of the Quadra-lateral table. They were all in heated debate. Debate however that was fueled by the theft of the Ball of Wisdom.

"You tardy chicken pot pie jock strap." one of the knights insulted pointing at another knight. "How could you let the Ball of Wisdom be stolen?"

"You're blaming me?" the other knight questioned.

"Gentlemen, Please!" King Alloicious cried attempting to restore order. "This is not a time to be divided. I'm sure everyone here understands the dangers, if the Ball of Wisdom has fallen into the wrong hands."

Everyone became silent reaching a mutual understanding that this was indeed not the time to be divided.

The King spoke again. "Now then, I have chosen Sir Osis of the Liver to find and retrieve the Ball of Wisdom."

The knights turned to Sir Osis of the Liver.

"With all due respect your majesty; I'm a very old and tired joke. Recovering the Ball of Wisdom would only be impractical for me and the kingdom." he explained.

"Very well." King Alloicious sighed.

He scanned the room looking for another knight to take Sir Osis of The Liver's place. King Alloicious then invested his attention into the Duke of Ellington.

"Ah yes, Duke of Ellington, my most trusted knight." he praised.

The Duke of Ellington raised his hand to interrupt the King.

"I'm sorry your majesty." he sighed. "I'm an outdated joke. Only a select few would understand, so I too would be impractical for this assignment."

"I will go." said a voice from behind the table.

"Who said that?" asked the King.

Emerging from the shadows was a girl. Her hair tied up, and wearing glasses, she confidently approached King Alloicious. Her name was Crystal.

"I did. My name is Crystal, and I will find the Ball of Wisdom." she proclaimed.

The Knights of the Quadra-lateral table all snickered to themselves. However, this was not out of earshot for Crystal. She looked back and gave them a glare, which only led to more laughter by the knights.

"Young lady, I assume this is just a dare someone put you up to?" asked King Alloicious. He himself also snickered as if this was some kind of joke.

"No, your majesty." replied Crystal. "With your permission, I will find the Ball of Wisdom."

"I don't think we can send you out." stated King Alloicious. "This isn't women's work."

Crystal restrained the urge to tell King Alloicious off. Instead she sighed heavily turning to walk away from the famed Quadra-lateral table.

"Wait." cried Merlin.

Crystal stopped in her tracks, after hearing Merlin. Her family was somewhat close to him. Sort of an Uncle Merlin. However more on her family later.

"Come on your Majesty; let her go find the Ball of Wisdom. Nobody else wants to find it, and besides it's not the 1370's anymore." he pleaded. "Besides that, haven't you heard of the Countess M.T.M.? All anybody saw of her was her legs, but she starred in several plays because of her brains."

King Alloicious thought for a few moments, while Crystal and everyone else in the room waited intently for his answer. For King Alloicious knew that if he sent Crystal, and if she failed, it would not only tarnish the honour of her own family, but it may lead the people to put his leadership as a king into question.

"What do I do?" he thought. "Let's see, if I send Crystal, it leads to 2 x 2 equals 4 multiplied by the coefficient of drag + (Parasite drag) + (Induced drag) divided by 1 horse of $E=MC2$ − (Xavier Cougat) x 3 and 1/2, in which Sarah buys 20 watermelons at 3 dollars a slice, which goes into the mass of a 3 dimensional object 50 times, which = Impeachment. Oh, to heck with it, I've got a son that can take over. It's not like he's going to leave the monarchy for Megan..."

"Very well." he sighed.

"But your majesty, you can't send a girl to find the Ball of Wisdom." protested one of the knights.

"So, you're going to go find the Ball of Wisdom?" asked King Alloicious.

The knight sighed heavily.

"No, I can't... My name is owned by Disney, and costs too much to use." he explained.

"Very well. Let the history books show that I, King Alloicious Robespierre Gaylord Arbuthnot Egbert..." The King inhaled deeply. "... Ickabagh Frobisher the 5th and eight sixteenths have sent a girl named Crystal to find the Ball of Wisdom." he decreed. "And I hope I haven't made a grave mistake." he thought to himself.

Crystal bowed thankfully.

"Thank you, your Majesty. I won't fail the Kingdom."

Crystal returned home, flushed with her success. Her mother Joan was waiting for her in the doorway.

"How did it go?" asked Joan.

"Well, it was a tough debate, but in the end the King realized I was the best choice to go find the Ball of Wisdom." Crystal explained radiating with pride.

"Merlin helped you out, didn't he?" Joan snickered.

Crystal sighed realizing that she really did owe this all to Merlin.

"Yes mom, he did...."

"I thought so." Joan chuckled. "But listen, I wouldn't trust anybody else except you to go find the Ball of Wisdom."

Crystal's mother had a warm and confidence building look. It was the kind of look that if she boxed it up, and gave it to you personally, you could accomplish anything.

"Thanks mom." smiled Crystal. "I better get ready to go."

Crystal then rushed up the stairs to her room.

"Crystal! Wait!" cried Joan.

"What?" Crystal replied halfway up the stairs.

Joan comically got on her knees.

"Before you go, please clean your room." she pleaded.

"Fine mom..." Crystal sighed. "I'll have it clean in three shakes of a lamb's tail."

"Tell you what, I'll give you six shakes of a lamb's tail." Joan bargained.

"Why six?" questioned Crystal.

Joan stood back up laughing.

"Crystal, I've seen your room. Trust me you'll need the three extra shakes of a lamb's tail."

"Ha, ha, you're funny mom." Laughed Crystal sarcastically.

"Don't sass me girl, I'm still your mother." Joan spoke sternly.

"Yes ma'am." saluted Crystal comically and she bolted away before her mother could say anything more.

Joan simply chuckled to herself. She knew from the day that Crystal was born that Crystal was no ordinary girl. In school while the other girls jumped rope at recess, Crystal would sneak off to the sword dueling grounds. There she would find a very large stick and take on the evilest looking practice battle dummy of the bunch.

She was caught numerous times, and numerous times "Uncle" Merlin would stand up for her, clearing her name. Like I said, Crystal is no ordinary girl, however she does know how to cook. Some would say that she is the best cook in the kingdom, but Crystal's sense of taste craved something more than woodstove top chicken soup. She craved the bittersweet taste of adventure.

Later that day Crystal was ready to embark on her search for the Ball of Wisdom. Her grandmother Margaret, as well as Joan, and Crystal's younger siblings, Anthony, Hugh, and Wyllo, were saying their farewells to her.

"Crystal, are you sure you don't want my carrot cake recipe for the journey?" asked Margaret.

"I'm sure Grandma. Thank you for offering." answered Crystal.

"All right. Be safe out there." Margaret said, as she placed the somewhat tattered recipe card back into her own jacket.

"I will Grandma." smiled Crystal.

Crystal then turned to her siblings and knelt down to be at their height.

"Crystal?" Anthony asked. "Can you get Hugh and I real armor and weapons?"

"You'll have to talk to mom about that one." smiled Crystal. "I can bring you home some Turkish delight though."

"You're not going to get us that cheap candy store stuff, are you?" asked Anthony.

"No. I'll get you and Hugh the real stuff."

"Equal portions?" Hugh chimed in.

"Yes, equal down to the last milligram." promised Crystal.

The boys shared a high five in delight, as Crystal went over to Wyllo, who was just sitting on the ground watching the world go by.

"Keep an eye on those two." Crystal pointed directing Wyllo's attention to Anthony and Hugh.

Wyllo responded by nodding demurely at Crystal, and then gave Crystal the biggest possible hug she could. When they eventually let go of each other, Crystal stood up and faced her somewhat proud Mother and Grandmother. They all looked at each other for a moment. Crystal then leapt into their arms giving them both a hug. She let go of them and climbed onto her horse.

"Bye mom, bye Grandma." she waved, as her horse began to trot away.

"Be back before supper tomorrow!" Joan called. "Grandma is making your favourite!"

"Also, Crystal!" Margaret shouted. "Don't do anything I wouldn't do! And if you do, make sure to cover it up with an inuendo joke from a G-rated Pixar film!"

With the sound advice and support of her family, Crystal and her noble steed galloped out of the Kingdom. Some in the Kingdom laughed. Some in the Kingdom were hopeful as she heard numerous comments being made.

"A girl? Out on a quest? What a preposterous notion."

"You can do it!"

However, Crystal didn't care what the people thought. Dear reader this is only the mere prep for our hero's long-awaited taste of bittersweet adventure.

To Be Continued...

Part Two

Crystal had searched far and wide across the land for the ball of wisdom. She knew very well that she could not return to the kingdom without it. She knew that by going on this quest, she had put her family's honour into question. Merlin thankfully was willing to give Crystal a hand with finding the ball of wisdom. He had provided Crystal with a magical device to help track where exactly the ball was being kept. All Crystal knew about the theft of the ball was that it was stolen by a creature, brown in colour, possibly a dragon.

All was mediocre in the land. Crystal rode her noble steed down the dirt pathway. Suddenly she heard a loud soprano voice cry out.

"DEAN! Ohhhh Dean! Where are you Dean?"

She stopped her horse in the middle of the path. Approaching her was a male fairy, with seemingly exaggerated movements.

"Hey, you! Yes you lady? Have you seen Dean?" he asked. The man bowed graciously to Crystal, then clumsily hit his head into the horse.

"Oh gee, I'm real sorry horsey." He apologized.

"No, I can't say I've seen anyone named Dean." Replied Crystal. The man frowned.

"Oh darn. Well listen, " If you find him can you please tell him... can you please tell him..." he repeated. "...That Fairy Lewis is lookin' for him?"

"Fairy Lewis was it?" asked Crystal checking with the man.

"Yes, ma'am that is I, Fairy Lewis. Biggest thing to hit France since the plague, har, har." Jokingly explained Fairy. "You know Dean, the one I'm lookin' for, well he and I are Pardners in an act. I'm what you'd call the Stooge, a Patsy of sorts, but gee I sure hope I find Dean. I even asked the Bellboy at the hotel to help me. You see, sometimes he drinks too much Dean. Not the Bellboy."

"Thank you for clarifying that." Nodded Crystal.

"Anyways, Dean becomes sort of childish. A kind of... kind of... hey lady do you have any words off the top of that pretty little head of yours?" he gestured to Crystal.

"He becomes sort of a Delicate Delinquent?"

"Yeah, yeah, one of those." Nodded Fairy somberly. "But boy I tell yeah, once we're done touring through Europe its Hollywood or Bust. Then we'll be Living It Up with the Artists and Models."

Fairy then whistled comically, making a clicking noise with his mouth, and polishing his fingernails on his shirt in a slow exaggerated fashion, all at the same time he was making extreme facial expressions to convey his shyness towards girls.

"Did you say something about a hotel?" asked Crystal as she noticed the quickly darkening sky.

"Just up this dirt road and on your left." Pointed Fairy. "However, you will keep a look out for Dean, won't you?"

"Of course, I will." Replied Crystal.

"Gee, you're a niceee lady."

"Thank you." Smiled Crystal.

"Anyways, I will continue to look for Dean, and I will let you on your way Madame. Remember, You're Never Too Young, and always protect The Family Jewels from the Disorderly Orderly."

The two parted ways. Fairy Lewis continued to look for Dean, and Crystal headed to the hotel for the night, where she would continue to look for the ball of wisdom. Crystal hitched up her horse to the post outside the hotel. It was a quaint modest looking building with a touch of old familiar British class. She walked through the old-style door, into the lobby, which was just as classy. She approached the desk, admiring its dark oak colour. A top the dark coloured desk was a shiny silver hotel bell. Crystal rang it once. No one answered. She rang it again. No one answered. She then smiled to herself mischievously, and then rang the bell repeatedly. Suddenly a bald man stood from under the desk. He stood tall with impeccable posture. He snatched the bell away from Crystal.

"Young lady, it is impolite to ring the bell more than three times." He spoke in a polite well-mannered British accent. "You have rung this bell exactly fifty-three and a half times."

"I'm sorry." Crystal frowned.

"Oh well no matter, you know for next time. You must be here about a room. I'm your host Mister Sinclair."

Mr. Sinclair then pulled out a large leather hotel logbook.

"Yes, I would just like a room for one night." Explained Crystal.

"All right. We have a room with a bath." He said, flipping through the logbook. "This room also has a rather comfy bed and overlooks the road."

"Yes, that will be all right." Nodded Crystal.

"Young lady, "That will be fine" is the proper way to say that statement, in this country."

Crystal was about to have enough of this over correcting snob, but instead restrained herself.

"My apologies. Please put the room under the name of Crystal."

"All right. I'll have Manuel show you to your room and help you with any baggage."

Mr. Sinclair then rang the bell exactly three times.

"You see young lady, exactly three times, hmmm." He smiled arrogantly.

The sound of the bell echoed through the hotel halls, and a short Spanish man with a moustache wearing a white shirt and black tie shuffled into the lobby quickly.

"Ah Manuel." Greeted Mr. Sinclair. "It's about time you showed up, you're tardy, I expect you to show up faster when you hear the bell ring. Anyways, no matter. This young lady needs some baggage taken to her room."

"Que?" replied Manuel.

Mr. Sinclair sighed heavily.

"Oh dear, I forgot you don't speak a speck of English."

"Que?"

"Just... just... give me one second."

Mr. Sinclair then ducked back under his desk and re-emerged with a Spanish to English dictionary. He flipped through it furiously for a few moments. Mr. Sinclair read through the book and proceeded to speak in the Spanish language. Unfortunately to Manuel it translated to,

"Manuel she is tardy, cover her in huevos and show her a good time, and please do handle her baggage."

Manuel thought for a moment about what Mr. Sinclair had said, and then looked at Crystal.

"Senior!" he gasped. "I... I... how you say? Can't."

"What... what... what do you mean you can't?" asked Mr. Sinclair, clearly irritated.

"Que?"

Mr. Sinclair was now turning red as a beet.

"WHAT-DO-YOU-MEAN-YOU-CAN'T?!?" he shouted. "TAKE -HER-BAGS-UP-TO-ROOM-3-2-3!"

"Ah Si Senior." Smiled Manuel. He started dancing a solo tango.

Crystal was in awe by the hotel staff's behaviour. She chose not to say anything but laughed to herself.

"RIGHT! ENOUGH!" shouted Mr. Sinclair as he slammed his fists on the desk. "Take her" He pointed at Crystal frantically. "Up" he pointed to the sky. "To room" he then pointed to his office. "3" he gestured on his right hand. "2-3! Comprende?!"

"Si." Nodded Manuel.

"Follow Senorita." Gestured Manuel.

With Manuel leading the way, Crystal followed close behind up the stairs of the hotel. They both walked down the hallway, until they reached Crystal's room. Manuel then turned to face Crystal.

"I must apologize for Mr. Sinclair's earlier behaviour." He said. "He can be quite a pain at times."

"Manuel? You can speak fluent English?" exclaimed Crystal.

"Sí." He smiled. "I just pretend to not be able to speak English just to irritate Mr. Sinclair. I learned from the best. A two-day seminar run by Sir Jonathan Cleese."

"I see, and I can understand." Nodded Crystal.

"You won't tell Mr. Sinclair, that I can speak English, will you?"

Crystal smiled at Manuel.

"Que?" she said.

"Thank you, Senorita." Smiled Manuel. "I also change the hotel sign from time to time. Have a good stay here, and if you can try and come down for supper. We'll be serving Waldorf salad."

He opened the room door for Crystal and handed her the key.

"Thank you, Manuel."

Manuel waved goodbye to Crystal as she entered the hotel room, shutting the door behind her. She admired the room, while walking over to her window to admire her view. Crystal looked out the window and saw Mr. Sinclair looking completely frantic, as he stood in front of the hotel sign.

"Watery Fowls?!?!" he shouted. "Who keeps doing this?!?!"

Crystal grinned widely and closed the drapes for the night.

The next morning Crystal awoke with a determination to get down to business. The business being, finding the ball of wisdom. She strolled down the hotel steps confidently. In her hand she held a piece of paper, which contained a picture of the ball of wisdom. She approached two old ladies, who were making their way to breakfast.

"Excuse me? Have you seen this ball?" asked Crystal.

The two ladies slid their spectacles closer to their eyes and examined the picture carefully.

"Oh, I must say that is a very lovely ball of wisdom." Commented one of the ladies.

"But I'm afraid we haven't seen it dearie." Added the other lady.

"That's all right." Nodded Crystal. "Thank you anyways."

Crystal let the two old ladies continue to breakfast. However, Crystal did not give up hope. All day she asked anyone and everyone she saw, if they had seen the ball of wisdom. Unfortunately, no one had seen it. Even Merlin's device was drawing a blank. After a full day of searching and asking questions, there were no answers, Crystal was now at the restaurant of the hotel. She had no idea what her next steps would be, until a man with finely polished buttons approached Crystal.

"I hear you've been looking for a ball of wisdom." The man said.

"I have." Replied Crystal. "Do you have something to do with its theft?"

"Quite quick to judge, aren't we? but, no." replied the man. "However, I may know who did."

Crystal diverted all her attention to the man with shiny buttons.

"A few nights ago, I was walking in the forest just over yonder." Explained the man. "When I saw a dragon, I didn't have anything to fight him, so I hid. He seemed nervous, almost talking to himself, like he had done something bad but he himself was trying to make it feel like the right thing. The dragon then uncurled it's claws, revealing an orb that glowed brightly. The air around me began to turn into a fierce wind, at which point I snuck away."

Crystal stood up quickly, almost excited. This was the first lead she had to where the ball of wisdom.

"Tell me sir, where was this forest?"

"Like I said, over yonder." His crooked finger pointed.

Any young girl who has taken geography and mapping knows that Yonder is approximately North West from one's current position. Crystal grabbed the man's hand and shook it wildly.

"Thank you, thank you."

With that Crystal rushed away.

"Hey!" the man cried. "Don't I get a tip for my tip?"

"Stay in school and eat healthy foods!" Crystal cried back.

She ran outside as quickly as possible, mounting her horse, galloping yonder.

It was a long night of travels. In the morning Crystal rode her noble steed through the forest. It was peaceful and quiet, as a calm gentle breeze wrapped itself around the surrounding mountains. She felt calm in this forest. She began riding up a hill, and as she got closer to the top of the hill, she began to see the top of a castle. More and more of the castle became visible as Crystal climbed to the top of the hill. When she reached the top of the hill however she saw that the castle was massive. Its size looming over the green countryside. Suddenly, the magical device that was in her bag started vibrating wildly. Crystal brought the device out of her bag which made it vibrate even more. Suddenly the calm gentle breeze that was blowing through the forest turned into a vicious wind that blew the trees in such a way that they pointed themselves in the direction of the castle. Crystal ordered her horse to charge at the castle. Soon the horse was galloping as fast as the wind. For a moment it had seemed like the wind had picked them up and carried them towards the castle.

As Crystal charged to the castle, she heard an odd cry. It was not the wind; it wasn't her horse. A dragon suddenly emerged from the castle entrance, the same dragon that had stolen the ball of wisdom. He was intimidating and scary. His long claws clutching the side of the castle, as he climbed to see Crystal galloping confidently towards him.

However, the dragon opened his mouth, revealing his sharp voracious fangs. This spooked the horse and Crystal was thrown to the ground, as her horse ran away in fear. Crystal was on her own now to fend off the dragon. She drew out her sword, getting right back up on her feet, ready to defend herself. The dragon charged, fiercely. He got closer and closer to Crystal. She knew deep down that she might not be able to survive the dragon's attack, but the driving force of adrenaline convinced her that she had to try and defeat this dragon. Crystal prepared to meet her maker. Although at the same time she was preparing to strike a crushing blow. Suddenly, the dragon stopped a few feet from her. With a stunned look, he fell to the ground. The magical device had blasted a charge that rendered the dragon unconscious.

Crystal walked over to the now docile dragon. She clutched her sword reluctantly and prepared to smite him. The dragon suddenly opened its eyes and looked at Crystal.

"Please... Don't...." The dragon murmured, seeming to beg for mercy.

Crystal saw something in the dragon's eyes. She saw a kind of human emotion and sensibility. She threw her sword off to the side, and began petting the dragon, attempting to soothe it. The dragon then slowly got up. Standing next to Crystal, the dragon didn't look as big. He wasn't small but he wasn't huge either. His fierce appearance had also disappeared.

"Why didn't you kill me?" he asked.

"I didn't want to." replied Crystal.

The two stared at each other awkwardly for a moment.

"Why are you here?" asked the dragon.

"I'm searching for the ball of wisdom. This magical device brought me here." Crystal replied showing the device to the creature.

"Oh, shiny." he commented gleefully. "I believe I have what you're looking for. Come with me."

Although Crystal had no reason to trust the dragon, she felt he could be trusted. She followed closely behind as he led the way. Both went through the front courtyard before entering the castle. Crystal saw bells, wind chimes, as well as other metal objects that shined and gleamed in the sunlight.

Crystal then sped up her pace so she could walk alongside the dragon.

"Why do you have all this stuff?" she asked.

The dragon responded with a small smile. "I like shiny things. I try to maintain their shine; it makes me happy."

"Surely a dragon like you must have a name, correct?" asked Crystal.

"Incorrect. I never had the need for one, so I guess I don't." he explained.

They arrived at the door that would lead to the main building of the castle. The dragon opened the door and held it open for Crystal. She smiled at his gentlemanly manner and walked inside. The door closed behind them. The interior of the castle was what could be expected for a creature of his size. Large hallways, and big doors. Several paintings lined these hallways. The paintings of course all had shiny gold frames. The dragon and Crystal walked down the hallway together. Then Crystal looked up at the dragon, as he walked beside her.

"You know something? I'm going to give you a name." She said.

"Why?" the dragon asked.

"Well because the narrator of this story keeps calling you, the dragon." explained Crystal. " Let's face it, that's pretty bland. I don't know what it is, but there's something about you. Therefore, I think you deserve a name."

"I'm flattered." The dragon smiled. "However, I am old. It is too late for me to have a name."

"Nonsense, you're never too old." assured Crystal.

"So, what are you going to name me?" he asked.

"I'll have to think about it." Crystal said, taking in every detail of him with her eyes.

The two reached the end of the hallway. They both stood at a large metal door.

"The Ball of wisdom is in here." he pointed, to the door. "In this room is where I keep my most prized possessions."

The dragon opened the door for Crystal. She walked into the room. Crystal's eyes widened as she saw that the room was filled with shelves and the shelves were filled with books. Hardcover, soft cover, fiction, non-fiction, and even sheet music. Crystal then saw in the center of the room on a pedestal, the ball of wisdom.

She was in awe, as the ball of wisdom was projecting its magic onto blank paper turning the plain white paper into a book. While at the same time, the ball of wisdom was constantly extracting knowledge from the various other books that line the shelves.

"I'm sorry I took your people's ball of wisdom." apologized the dragon.

"Why did you take it?" asked Crystal.

"I've been alone for a long time. I wanted to learn about humans, I felt that somehow at some time I was a part of your people." explained the dragon. "One of my books said that a ball of wisdom existed. I realized that if I found the ball, I might understand humans, before actually having to meet one because I'm just not socially ready yet. Then maybe I could become their friend, and maybe even understand myself as well."

"But if you wanted to become a friend of humans, why did you attack me?" asked Crystal.

"Because I learned about humans, the ball of wisdom informed me that taking their ball of wisdom was a crime in the human's eyes, and that I would be punished. Since I'm vastly different, so different that I may be feared, I believed I would be killed." explained the dragon. "In lay man's terms your species violent tendencies bothered me deeply."

"If you fear humans, why trust me? Why bring me into your castle to the room where you keep your most prized possessions?" Crystal asked.

"You know, you ask a lot of questions." chuckled the dragon.

"It's the only sure-fire way I know to get answers." smiled Crystal.

"Well, I could ask you the same question about you trusting me. However, you did not wish to kill me, you even want to give me a name. It does not take a ball of wisdom for me to realize that you are different from the rest." Explained the dragon.

Crystal felt flattered to some degree. "Well I'd say you're pretty different from the kind you come from as well."

"I'll take that as a compliment." shrugged the dragon.

"You should." smiled Crystal. "Being different is not a bad thing, it's a great thing."

The dragon smiled at Crystal and Crystal smiled back.

"I guess I should return what isn't mine." stated the dragon.

"Yes, it was not right to take it without asking, but I've got another question." Crystal chuckled. "How are you using this to learn?"

"Well you've already seen it in action. As you've probably noticed I like to read, and I feel I can better process the knowledge if it is in the format of a book." explained the dragon.

"Interesting." Crystal said, as the ball of wisdom wrote another book. She stood completely mesmerized by the process.

The ball of wisdom finished the book, and with that the dragon picked up the ball of wisdom in his claws.

"I'll return it personally, as long as you come with me, and help me explain to your people why I took it and that I'm sorry." offered the dragon.

"Sure thing." smiled Crystal. "I'll put in a good word for you."

They walked out of the castle into the front courtyard. the wind was blowing in such a way the shiny bells were making a beautiful noise.

"I'm sorry about scaring off your horse." the dragon apologized.

"It's okay." Crystal said. "It was a rental anyways."

"If you get on my back, we can fly back to the kingdom." suggested the dragon.

"You can fly?" asked Crystal as she climbed on his back.

"Well I never had a reason to, until now. So, I guess so."

The dragon began concentrating heavily, as Crystal could feel they were slowly rising off the ground. The dragon beamed confidently as his wings followed the principle of Bernoulli.

"Thank you for flying Air Dragon. We will be serving your meal shortly. In the event of an emergency, there are exits here, here, and here."

Crystal smiled and laughed. Soon they were off and flying back to the kingdom to return the ball of wisdom. Crystal and the Dragon flew, heading back to the Kingdom. Crystal and the dragon during this flight had found something in common, riddles.

"A riddle for you." Crystal said.

"I'm listening." The dragon said as he flew avoiding a lost migrating flock of Canada geese.

"What do you get when you cross a shark and Jack frost together?"

The dragon thought of every possible solution to the joke.

"I'm just drawing blanks on this one." he replied.

"Frost bite." Crystal laughed.

The Dragon laughed as well, causing the flight to be a bit bumpy.

"How far is it to your kingdom?" asked the dragon.

"It's just over there." Crystal pointed.

Sure enough, the kingdom was in view of both Crystal and the dragon. The dragon then flew at double time speed. When they arrived, they touched down at the center of the kingdom. However, the kingdom was completely abandoned. It was eerily quiet, as a tumble weed blew through the now empty marketplace.

"Where is everyone?" asked Crystal, who was clearly worried by the uneasy quiet and lack of people.

"Maybe they all went out for Chinese." The dragon joked, trying to add levity to a very unusual situation.

"That would be pretty hard to do, since in these times the nearest Chinese restaurant is in China, and I'm pretty sure they've got some dynasty changeover going on right now." replied Crystal.

"Ah yes, they seem to have one every hundred years or so. First it was the Ming dynasty, then the Ying, and then the Yang, and then the Dang, but these days who's keeping track?" the dragon asked.

"You seem to be." chuckled Crystal. "However, that still doesn't answer the question, where is everybody?"

The dragon and Crystal looked around the kingdom, and there was no sign of anyone. However, objects and households looked to be completely untouched.

"An entire populous of a kingdom doesn't just disappear into thin air." commented the dragon.

"Not normally." replied Crystal. "This is getting quite worrying, my family, and my friends, gone... where could they be?"

"I can tell you where they are." said a strange old voice.

Out of the shadows a stereo typical old man with a stereo typically strange junk cart emerged from the shadows.

"Who are you?" asked Crystal.

"My identity to you is irrelevant, because I am merely here for the purposes of the plot." answered the old man. "What is really of relevance to you, is that I have information of what happened to the people of this kingdom. I have information of what happened to your family and friends. Do you believe me, Crystal?"

Crystal was now becoming exceedingly worried and frightened. Especially since they had never met and yet the old man knew her name.

"Listen sir." the dragon reasoned. "You're kind of freaking us out, and Crystal here who you strangely know her name even though it's clear you two have never met, would just like to know where the people of this kingdom are, and quite frankly I want to know too."

"So, you want to know where the people of the kingdom are?" the old man asked.

"Okay, can you please just tell us? You beat around the bush worse than a weed whacker." Crystal said.

The old man raised his hand and pointed to the East.

"The Land of Fairies."

The Dragon looked at Crystal, looking to her for their next move. "Well Crystal?"

"Let's roll." Crystal said jumping on thee dragon's back.

Crystal and the dragon took flight yet again, heading for the land of fairies. The old man stayed behind but disappeared as mysteriously as he had appeared.

To Be Continued...

Part Three

When we last left our heroes, they were flying to the land of fairies. Their reasoning for this was since everyone in the kingdom in which Crystal resided had disappeared. "I hope we can find everyone." commented Crystal, as she brushed her hair out of her eyes as the wind had blown it there in the first place.

"I hope so too Crystal." The dragon replied.

"Is that the land of Fairies up ahead?" pointed Crystal.

"I would assume so. I'll set a course." The dragon replied.

The Dragon flew faster, as the Land of Fairies drew closer. The Land of Fairies was embedded on a mountainside, surrounded by waterfalls. The dragon touched down lightly between the waterfalls. Crystal shielded herself from the spraying mist. They both examined the area. There was a small stone shack, a top a foothill. The dragon and Crystal hiked up to the door. They saw that the door had shiny silver chimes, and a sign that read, "Please ring for service".

"Can I please ring them?" asked the dragon. "They look amazing."

"Go ahead." Giggled Crystal.

The dragon rang the chimes. Suddenly out of nowhere, yellow sparkling dust appeared, and so did a man. The man wore a bright green suit, while having a mischievous but trustworthy smile.

"Ah, top of the afternoon to ya'. My name is Seán. That's spelled S-E-A-N, and please don't forget the Irish Fada accent over the A. How can I be of service to ya'?" He said greeting with a heavy Irish accent. "You know the union, they probably won't let me do this, but we're havin' a special on three wishes. Three for the price of one."

"We're havin' a special on three wishes. Three for the price of one."

"Well my name is Crystal and thank you but no." Crystal said. "However, we are looking for the populous of a kingdom."

"Oh, are ya' now, and where would one find said populous of said kingdom?" asked Seán.

"That's what we're trying to figure out." The Dragon added. "We were told the people would be here."

Seán began to smile widely.

"Ah I see, you were sent by the referral service." Then Seán laughed. "I told that Amber that getting a referral service would help business but trying to convince her to do anything is like trying to tell a Scotsman to stop playing his bagpipes."

"Well an old man sent us." Crystal explained. "Was he part of the referral service?"

"Did he happen to give you a name?" Seán asked.

"No." answered the dragon.

"Oh dear. That doesn't sound like anybody from the service I picked." explained Seán with a confused look on his face. "They always give out a name, simply because they want you to take the survey for how the referral went."

"Well this isn't helping; the kingdom is still missing." Commented the dragon.

"You say an old man sent you here?" asked Seán. "As well as the fact that the people of your kingdom have disappeared?"

"Yes." Crystal's answer sounded quite frantic.

"Calm down lass. I just hung some kilts out to dry; I wouldn't want them to get stressed, wool and all that. I just must go inside the shack for a moment and see what I can do for ya'."

Seán then retreated into the shack.

"Do you think this guy knows anything about what happened to everybody?" Asked the dragon.

"Well..." Crystal surmised. "We don't have much to go on, and Seán seems to be our only..."

"Matthew!!!"

Crystal had been interrupted by Seán, who at that moment was inside the shack. His loud Irish voice had somehow managed to stay outside.

"We've got customers!!! Open the cave!!!" ordered Seán.

Suddenly one of the waterfalls split into two revealing a large cave, with potions, wands and spell books. Seán then came out of the shack.

"Ok, let's see if we can find that kingdom for ya' now."

"Am I going to fit in that cave?" asked the dragon.

"Oh, don't worry, you're a big fella but I think you'll be fine." replied Seán.

For the dragon, the cave was a tight squeeze, and a book or two was knocked over, but the dragon found there was more space further down.

"Wait a minute." Crystal said, listening intently. "Is that Irish fiddle music?"

"Indeed, it is." beamed Seán. "The best kind of music for the back story of a hopeful Irishman."

As they all walked through the cave, Seán began to tell his life story.

"You know, I never used to work here. I was a leprechaun over in Dublin, but that job got kind of boring. Really all I was doin' was guarding pots of gold. Not much of a way to spend a life, if you ask me."

The Dragon and Crystal had no choice but to listen to Seán. However, they seemed interested in his story.

"So, the good Lord brought me here, and an angel met me here saying I should seek out employment."

"But you are a man?" asked the dragon.

"My, aren't you a perceptive one, what gave it away? The lack of feminine body parts? Or maybe it was my 5 o'clock shadow?" Seán asked sarcastically.

"I'm sorry I didn't mean to offend you, but with your gender being the way it is, why work in the Land of Fairies?"

"When I first applied here, they turned me down." Seán explained. "I had the magic abilities they were looking for, and most importantly I had the people skills. Believe you me, the people skills are the most important part of this job. I have to know how to handle the people that use their third wish to ask for three more wishes, when they can't. Against policy and all that."

"So how did you get this job?" asked Crystal.

"Well the people that used to run this place, they told me flat out that they couldn't hire me because I was a man. I'll tell you two something', folk lore is quite gender biased. So anyways, I brought my case to the equal rights board of mythical creatures, and sure enough they saw my side, and here I am today."

"That's quite the story of fighting for equal rights." admired Crystal.

"I like to think that I made a difference in this world for the good." Seán smiled. "If you want to take some advice from a rebellious leprechaun from Dublin, whatever idea that is in your brain that you think will change the world for the good, stop thinkin' about it, and do it."

The dragon and Crystal took Seán's words of wisdom into consideration. Eventually they all finally reached the end of the hallway. There was a wall, and on that wall was a large slightly discoloured map of the world.

"Here we can find your kingdom. It's a map of the known world." explained Seán. He then handed Crystal a dart. "Hold this dart, then throw it at the map wherever it lands that's where your kingdom be. I know it's an unorthodox method, but I've used this before. From wallets to keys, I've found them."

Crystal gripped the dart hoping for the best. The dragon was also hoping for the best. Crystal threw the dart. The dart whizzed through the air and landed outside the map, embedding itself into the rocky wall.

"Oh no." Seán murmured.

"Well that didn't work." The Dragon stated bluntly.

"My dear creature. It is not a matter that the method did not work, it did work." explained Seán. "I said it was a map of the known world.

The dart has landed outside the map which is the unknown world. Your people are in the unknown."

"What do we do now?" asked Crystal.

"I don't know lass, but what's frightening is that there is only one type of people that are known to live in the unknown, The Ministry."

"Should you ask, or should I?" The dragon asked Crystal.

"Let's ask together."

"Who is The Ministry?" The dragon and Crystal asked together.

"An evil group of shape shifting demons." shuddered Seán. "They think the world should be ruled their way and not anybody else's. Unfortunately, their way of ruling involves stripping away a person's right to innocence, and other not nice things. The people of your kingdom must have something that the Ministry wants, desperately."

"Could it be the Ball of Wisdom?" whispered the dragon.

"You have a Ball of Wisdom?" asked Seán who had heard the dragon. "You know, that's information I could've used when ya' got here."

"We're sorry we didn't tell you." apologized Crystal. "We didn't think it mattered."

"Oh, kind girl, it does matter. You see, the Ministry needs that ball of wisdom to take over every kingdom, every commercial magical business, and every person." explained Seán.

"Oh no." Crystal shuddered.

"However, they need something I have, to complete their plan." Seán said. "So just another quick little story. My cousin Michael owns a pub in Scotland, and in the back room is a closet. I call it the closet of knowledge. It's a vast array of books. The Ball of wisdom utilizes books to make new books. Books of goodness in the hands of a good person..." Seán then lowered his voice to a sinister level of sound. "Books of evil, in the hands of an evil person."

"Interesting." Crystal commented.

"Yes, very interesting." A strange feminine voice said from behind them. "Now if you wouldn't mind, we'd like the Ball of Wisdom, so we can rule the world."

"Stand fast lads, it's one of the Ministry's cronies. Just follow my lead." explained Seán.

The Ministry woman snapped her fingers. A bright evil flame engulfed her, as she transformed into a fierce demon like creature.

Seán then snapped his fingers. All that happened was the Celtic music became louder. Seán walked slowly in front of the demon. He began tapping his feet on the ground, moving in a slow and rhythmic fashion. Each tapping sound that Seán's feet made echoed through the cave. Seán began to build up to a River Dance, dancing in circles around the demon. Crystal and the dragon observed Seán and his tactics, fearing that this was the end. The demon laughed to herself thinking that this would be easier than she had originally thought. The music tempo increased as Seán moved his feat faster, his tapping noises becoming more musical.

"Crystal, I say we get jiggy with it." The dragon smiled.

"Agreed." Crystal nodded.

The dragon extended his arm and Crystal grabbed hold, as they became partners for an Irish jig dance off.

Wait a minute, is that Ashley MacIssac? Whoa, when did we get the budget that we could get him to do a cameo appearance in this story? Sorry about my surprise... I wasn't expecting him.

Anyways with Ashley MacIssac standing in the background playing his fiddle, Seán began to dance wildly, with incredibly precise motions. He moved his feet in such a way that it confused the demon. The demon decided to not bother with Seán anymore, charging at Crystal instead. It came closer and closer. Just before he hit Crystal however, the dragon lifted her up in time with the music. The demon missed and hit the cave wall. Seán went over to the dazed demon and began to River Dance on its back. Crystal and the dragon continued to dance with the music having a joyous time. For a moment, both had forgotten they were battling a demon. In that moment the dragon realized that he liked dancing with Crystal. He liked seeing her smile and having a good time.

After three bars of music had passed the demon awoke ready to take another shot at them. Seán did his best to knock the demon out again. Unfortunately, it had recovered fully, throwing Seán to the ground. It began to charge at Crystal and the dragon who were still dancing.

"Look out!" Seán cried, to Crystal and the dragon.

Crystal and the dragon danced like never before. They jumped over the demon, then over again. Crystal then held her hands out for the dragon to grab. With his claws he awkwardly grabbed her hands. They then began to spin around in time with the music. They spun so fast that the demon was losing its concentration on her task. Crystal and the dragon began laughing out loud joyously. Seán employing a little bit of magic cast a spell that gave Crystal and the dragon each their own set of bright green River Dancing tap shoes. The demon encircled them one last time. Closer and closer the demon drew. As the music climaxed, Seán continued to provide a steady and precise beat that could be followed. He leaped through the air gracefully, clicking his heels together. The noise confused the demon even more. As Crystal and the dragon continued to dance, Seán joined them. As a group they became synchronized, dancing in true Irish style. The musical tapping noise of their feet weakened the demon even more. With a crushing blow the dragon swung his tale, clobbering the demon. The demon was unconscious. The music had ended. Crystal and the dragon bowed together.

"Bravo, bravo." applauded Seán. "I haven't seen dancing' like that since my cousin Maggie took first place in the Highland Games."

"And would you believe we never had a lesson in our lives?" joked the dragon. Crystal giggled in amusement.

"Oh, I would believe it." chuckled Seán. "However, that was some mighty fine dancing for a couple of beginners."

"Thank you, thank you." Crystal bowed again.

After all was said and done, the group gathered around the demon who had now regressed back to her human form. She then opened her eyes suddenly. The group became frightened as her eyes were now blood red.

"The Ministry will control all." She said in an old rough frightening tone of voice. "Crystal, we have your family. Bring the ball of wisdom to us, and we will return them, and if you don't well... Mwahahahahahahahahahahahahahahahahahaha!!!!" The demon laughed maniacally as she disappeared completely in a burst of flames.

Crystal was almost in tears. The dragon did his best to hold Crystal close and comfort her.

"Listen, Ms. Crystal, we will find your family, we will find your kingdom. However, the Ministry will now try to get the closet of knowledge, I suggest we go to the pub and protect it. When the Ministry does arrive, we'll get their damned crony to tell us where everyone is." Seán explained courageously.

Crystal nodded. She now realized that this had become a much more serious situation. "Hop on the dragon's back Seán and point us in the right direction."

To Be Continued...

Part Four

D ear reader, you are now four parts into this story. You deserve a re-cap.

Take a deep breath in and go.

So, there's this kingdom, and this magical little orb called the Ball of Wisdom. Basically, an orb with a large amount of knowledge. This orb was stolen by a dragon. The only person in the kingdom willing to go find it, was a young girl by the name of Crystal. Crystal eventually did find the ball of wisdom, as well as confronting the dragon that had stolen it. After some minor misunderstandings, the dragon and Crystal became friends and set out to return the ball of wisdom to Crystal's kingdom. However, when they returned to the kingdom, everyone had vanished. Due to a tip off, Crystal and the dragon ended up at the land of fairies, where they meet Seán. Seán is leprechaun turned fairy from Dublin. He offers to help Crystal and the dragon find the kingdom's people. After some magic bippity boppity, it is learned that the people are in the unknown world, where only an evil organization intent on ruling all the known world resides. The evil organization called the Ministry needs the ball of wisdom and the closet of knowledge to complete their goal of ruling overall.

Seán then teaches us all how to deal with an evil shape shifting demon, Riverdance the heck out of them. A beaten-up demon then threatens Crystal that the Ministry has her family, and that if Crystal does not give up the Ball of Wisdom harm may come to her family.

And now the continuation...

*Phew

Crystal, the dragon, and now Seán were flying to Scotland in the hopes of getting to the closet of knowledge before the Ministry.

"It's going to be a while before we get to Scotland, so I think I'll catch a few winks." yawned Seán. He then sprawled out on the dragon's back and fell asleep.

"So, how do you feel about your family being taken by the Ministry?' The dragon asked Crystal.

"Avocado." She replied.

"Say what, now?" questioned the dragon.

"Avocado. I just want to change the subject." explained Crystal. "Like don't get me wrong or anything, this is serious it's just that I don't want to talk about it right now."

"Okay, avocado it is." The dragon said. "In fact, if we are talking and we want to change the subject, all one of us has to do is say, avocado, and the subject shall be changed."

"Sounds reasonable." smiled Crystal.

Complete awkward silence then made itself present. Except for Seán, as he began talking in his sleep.

"Ack lads. They may take our women, they may take our land, but they will not take our FREEDOM!!!" He shouted in a rough Scottish accent.

"Is he reciting Braveheart?" The dragon snickered.

"To be honest I don't know." replied Crystal. "It's certainly some sort of Scottish battle cry."

Seán's talking in his sleep was just the catalyst needed to start Crystal and the dragon off on a long and interesting conversation. The dragon liked this. It had been many years since, he had anyone that he could talk to and have interesting but weird conversations with. To some extent the dragon could tell that Crystal liked talking to him as well, which was not far from the truth. There had been times when she did feel alone in the kingdom. Feeling invisible to her peers, unless she was the brunt of a joke. Because of this she would rather feel invisible. However, the dragon noticed her, and she noticed the dragon.

"Tropical Fish, what do you think about them?" asked Crystal, out of the blue.

The dragon laughed in confusion. "Well... they're wet, tropical, and fishy."

"Yes, yes they are." laughed Crystal.

The dragon and Crystal's laughter was so loud and joyful that it woke Seán.

"Are we there yet?" he yawned as he stretched, and his Irish accent returned.

"Almost." the dragon replied. "Which road are we taking the high road or the low road?"

"Just give me a moment." Seán said pulling out his road map.

He examined the map for a long while. He then scratched his head in confusion.

"I don't quite remember which way to go. It doesn't say here on my map. Maybe we take the low road? Or is it the high road? No, no I'm almost certain it's the low road. Wait a minute let me see if I remember the poem that was taught to me, so I'd remember. You take the high road and I'll take the low road and I'll be in Scotland before ye'."

"Seán just pick a road, or I'll pick it for us." the dragon threatened.

"I think we'd be better off if we did leave it up to chance." Seán surmised.

"Fair enough." The dragon said, as he turned to go up the high road.

It's probably a good or bad time to mention (depending on your perspective of the story) that the dragon is terrible at directions. However, on the bright side they all had quite a nice time in Moscow.

So, while our heroes are winging their way back to Scotland, I take you to the Unknown, to the castle of the Ministry. Two demons in the forms of man and a woman were plotting evil.

"I need a report on how our hostages are doing." Said the woman in the shadows.

"Sandi, they don't suspect anything. They still think they are in their own kingdom." The man smiled.

"Excellent love. Any news on getting the Ball of Wisdom into our possession?"

"Dean!!!" cried Fairy Lewis from down the hall.

"The worker, she failed." The man said becoming visibly nervous.

"The message was delivered to young Crystal?" asked Sandi.

"Dean!!!" Fairy cried again.

"Yes. We have reason to believe they are heading to the closet of knowledge."

Sandi tapped her long fingernails on a nearby table. She seemed frustrated.

"Send out another worker to apprehend the closet of knowledge. It's quite possible that young Crystal will be there too. Order the worker to apprehend her as well, by means of possession." Sandi then smiled an unnatural evil grin, even dentists feared this type of toothy smile.

"Ohhhh Dean!!!"

Sandi was now very irritated.

"Who on Earth keeps saying that?" she asked.

In crawled Fairy Lewis through the door on his hands and knees.

"Have any of you two seen Dean? I seem to have misplaced him in the known world." he said as he crawled all over the floor closely examining it for clues.

"Then why must you insist on looking for him here in the unknown?" asked Sandi.

"The light is better out here." Fairy said as straight faced as possible. "Gee lady, you certainly walked into that one." he said as he crawled to her feet, then looked at Sandi, standing above him. "Yeesh..." he exclaimed, responding to the look of her face.

"Could I please continue?" fumed Sandi.

"Oh, sure lady, just pretend like I'm not even here." Fairy continued to examine everything looking for Dean.

"Now as 1 was saying, 1 want you to bring Crystal's grandmother, the one they call Margaret to me, as well as her mother, the one they call Joan." She ordered

"You know 1 have a grandmother." interrupted Fairy Lewis. "And 1 have mother, of course that goes without saying. That would be ridiculous having a grandmother, without having a mother, mind you 1 would also need a father to exist, and my father's mother could also be my grandmother, which is the grandmother I'm talking about, you see."

Sandi inhaled deeply and counted to ten.

"Are you finished?" she asked.

"I'm just getting warmed up." nodded Fairy. "But it looks like I'm interrupting something, so 1 will leave. Maaaa!!! 1 finally met a nice laaady you can have coffee with."

Fairy Lewis then disappeared into a puff of smoke.

"You have your orders." Sandi said sternly to the man.

The man nodded in compliance and slithered out of the room.

Meanwhile in the fake kingdom, Margaret was walking through the marketplace with her daughter Joan. The marketplace was busy, as everyone was buying food and equipment for the week. It was full of laughter and the stereotypical question,

"How's the family?"

Margaret on the other hand, seemed to be the opposite of everyone else. Joan took notice that something was obviously bothering her mother.

"Mom what's wrong? You seem to be on edge." she asked.

"I'm worried about Crystal and her quest." replied Margaret.

"1 too am worried about Crystal." sighed Joan.

"It's not just that." Margaret lowered her voice to just above a whisper. "Things have been a little off here lately."

"What kind of "off" caliber are we talking about exactly?" asked Joan. "Is it Twilight Zone "off" caliber? Or psychedelic Johnny Depp "off" caliber?"

"Definitely psychedelic Johnny Depp." Replied Margaret without hesitation. "Just lots of the loathing and none of the fear. No one seems worried about Crystal, or the ball of wisdom anymore... it's odd... Nobody is searching anymore..."

"How about we start a little search party of our own?" smiled Joan maliciously.

Margaret frowned at Joan.

"Joan, that is against the rules set by our king." she stated in a serious tone. Her tone then lightened considerably. "Let's do it. It's nice to know that there is no doubt you are my daughter."

Margaret and Joan spent the rest of that day getting ready to find Crystal. Meanwhile Crystal, Seán and the Dragon had finally made it to Michael's pub in Scotland.

"We are here comrades." The dragon spoke in a heavy Russian accent.

"Is he going to be talking like this now for the entire adventure?" Crystal asked Seán.

Seán looked at Crystal and smiled. "I think so Comrade Crystal."

"Oh no." laughed Crystal.

They landed just in front of the pub. It was a massive tree. The likes of which Crystal had never seen before. Long branches extended themselves from the base of the trunk, curling and twisting into the night sky. They could hear the loud noise of people doing a Scottish drinking game.

39

Seán and Crystal disembarked the dragon, and headed into the pub. The dragon was about to head in himself until Seán stopped him.

"Easy there comrade dragon." He said, still having his Russian accent. "I think you might be a little big for glorious people's pub."

"Fair enough comrade, I will stay out here and stand guard."

Seán was glad that the dragon understood.

"Come Crystal, let us go into glorious people's pub."

As soon as Seán opened the door to enter, they were blasted immediately with the sound of bagpipe music and the smell of haggis. As the Scottish culture sank in, Seán began to lose his gruff Russian demeaner. He looked over to the man behind the bar. The man was quite brawny wearing his tartan patterned kilt, and it looked like he had been in a few fights in his time. A tough fighter but had the look of an angel.

"Michael!" Seán shouted to the man behind the bar. It was also clear that Seán had returned to his normal hyperactive Irish self.

"Ack, Seán me Cousin, how are things in Fairy land?" Michael asked with a manly Scottish accent.

"Well, that's actually why we're here." Seán then lowered his voice. "We need to see the Closet of Knowledge..."

"Aye, and who might this young lass be?" asked Michael as he pointed at Crystal.

"Oh, this young lass be Crystal." Seán introduced.

"Pleasure to meet you Michael." Crystal smiled.

"The pleasure is all mine lass." replied Michael, doing his best to flash whatever charm he could muster. "You're a pretty little thing. I'm in a band, you know."

Crystal smiled awkwardly, then walked away from Michael.

"Michael!" Seán said, clearly mad at his cousin. "Cool your damn blood pudding'. We have more pressing matters."

"Ack, and what kind of pressing matter would that be?" scoffed Michael.

"The Ministry, Michael." Seán was now straight faced and serious.

The name alone, to Michael, sounded so frightening that along with his skin tone, his kilt became pale.

"Scots Wha-hae!" The crowd cheered joyfully, as they danced to a jig being played by the piper.

The dragon who had heard this from outside began looking through the window. He then started to admire Crystal as she admired the design of the pub. Crystal then noticed that the dragon was looking at her, she waved and smiled demurely at him. However, the dragon, realizing that he had been caught looking at her, disappeared awkwardly from the window. He felt something for her, but he didn't know what that feeling was.

"Lass... Crystal." Michael called out. "I apologize for my earlier behavior. I will take you and Seán to the Closet of Knowledge."

"Apology accepted." smiled Crystal.

Crystal then followed Seán and Michael to a door in the back room. Michael then pulled out a key and so did Seán. They put their keys in at the same time. The door opened with an irritating creak.

"Hmmm... I might have to use a little WD-40 on those hinges." Michael surmised.

There was a long dark hallway behind the door.

"Looks like you'll need a little light." Seán said. He snapped his fingers. The rows of torches magically lit up one by one. Michael then gestured to Crystal.

"Lassies first." he said.

"Thank you." nodded Crystal.

Crystal walked into the dimly lit hallway.

"How far is it to the closet?" she asked.

"Not very far." answered Seán.

They walked for a few metres, or for a few feet, depending on whether you measure with metric or imperial standards. Eventually they arrived at a large old wooden door. Michael knocked three times on the door.

"Who goes there?" asked a voice from the other side.

"Ack, it is I, Michael, with Cousin Seán, and Crystal."

"What's the musical password?" The voice asked.

"Lad, you know damn right well it's me."

"Nope sorry, can't say I do. Unless I hear the musical password." insisted the voice.

"Fine." Michael sighed.

Then, from his sporran, Michael pulled out a tiny set of bagpipes. The bagpipes, once out of the sporran, began to enlarge to their normal size, revealing the colourful tartan bag as well as the deep dark blackwood drones.

"I wasn't lying when I said I was in a band." he smiled.

"Yes Michael, we know you're just trying to promote your rock band Scotch on the Rocks." sighed Seán.

Michael inflated the bag and struck up the drones. The bagpipes, which were perfectly tuned, made an iconic and unforgettable sound that gave Crystal goosebumps. He then began to play the tune that most Englishmen feared, Scotland The Brave.

"Hmmm... Scotland The Brave..." The voice said once Michael had finished. "Sorry, too common, everyone knows that tune."

"Dammit Sir Nectarine, I swear if you don't open this-" Michael said furiously.

"All right, all right I was only kidding." chuckled Sir Nectarine.

Michael stepped back from the door, as it opened wide. Inside was a majesty of books. It was so vast that it made the dragon's collection look like an underfunded elementary school library. The mere sight of the books and the various maps, and contraptions was enough to make Crystal salivate, just a little bit.

"Sir Nectarine! Where are ye'?" Michael called out.

The group of three was suddenly approached by a small 4-inch teddy bear, that was coloured like a nectarine, and moved with precise discipline.

"Sir Nectarine at your service, sir." He saluted. "Seán, what a pleasant surprise."

"Lad you know Seán and you know me, but this young lass is Crystal."

Sir Nectarine graciously bowed towards Crystal. "M'lady."

"Pleased to meet you." greeted Crystal. "Wait a minute, aren't you in another story?"

"Yes, but it hasn't been written in for some time. A teddy bear's got to make a living at something."

"Ack yes, that's why I hired him on to guard the Closet of Knowledge." explained Michael. "However, I must warn ye' don't let his appearance fool you. He may look cute but he's a tough fighter and a cracker jack guard."

"You got it boss." Sir Nectarine smiled.

"So, nothing is missing? and everything has been quiet?" asked Seán.

"Yes, sir." Sir Nectarine saluted.

"Ack, Seán why did you say your visit had something to do with the Ministry?" asked Michael.

Suddenly Sir Nectarine looked at Seán with a surprised look. "I'm sorry, did you say The Ministry?"

"Yes" replied Seán. "You see, they've kidnapped everyone from Crystal's kingdom, because they want the Ball of Wisdom."

"Ack, please tell me you have the Ball of Wisdom all safe and sound." Michael pleaded.

"Right here." Crystal said as she pulled out the orb from her bag.

The books within the Closet of Knowledge began to shake as they began to feel the presence of the ball. Said ball was also glowing brightly.

"There's a lot of power here." commented Sir Nectarine. "I can see why the Ministry wants the Ball of Wisdom, and the Closet of Knowledge. They'll stop at nothing to get these things."

"Exactly. We think that the Ministry will show up here to get the Closet of Knowledge. We plan to trap the demon they send and rescue the kingdom." explained Seán.

"Sounds like a job that will take all night." commented Michael. "Sir Nectarine, you're at high alert. Don't let your guard down for a second. We should also leave the Ball of Wisdom down here."

Crystal then gave the Ball of Wisdom to Sir Nectarine.

"Okay Michael, you've got Sir Nectarine doin' that, I assume we'll be guarding out front." Seán said.

"Ack yes we will. Also, I have some private accommodations where Crystal can spend the night and rest up." Offered Michael.

"Thank you, Michael. Also, there is a small matter of a large dragon, he's our other companion." explained Crystal.

"Not a problem at all lass." Michael said. "From time to time a giant will show up here, so I've got some larger accommodations around back."

Michael, Seán, and Crystal made there way back out to the pub, where everyone was laughing and dancing to Scottish folk tunes as well as Irish tunes. It was the kind of noise you would expect at a quaint pub in the middle of the Highlands.

"I think I'll turn in for the night." yawned Crystal.

"Just right up those stairs lass." pointed Michael.

Crystal began climbing the stairs to her room. It wasn't until then she realized just how tired she was, as she struggled to climb each step. The music and laughter began to fade as she entered the room.

"Hmmm... Early Elf Provincial, what an interesting decorating choice." She commented to herself.

Crystal changed out of her old clothes, and into a white satin night gown that was inside the normal room closet. It dragged slightly on the floor when she wore it, but it was better than nothing. She untied her hair, which seemed like it couldn't wait to escape the confines of her hair elastic. The length of her dark hair rushed to her shoulders. She then looked around the room more closely, noticing that her room had drapes. She parted the drapes to reveal that she also had a quaint, simple balcony. Crystal opened the balcony doors and stepped outside into the cool Scottish air. The dragon was just below her. When he heard the door open, he stood up which made his head come up to balcony level.

"I almost thought you had forgotten about me." he said. "Which is fine... because I don't really do the whole crowd social thing."

"Don't worry, we didn't. Also, I'm glad you're back to your old self." smiled Crystal.

"Yes. The Russian version of me was getting kind of annoying." the dragon laughed.

Crystal then gestured to around back.

"There's a place to sleep for you over there."

"Thank you." nodded the dragon. He didn't move though, he wanted to stay with Crystal, just a little while longer.

"I have never seen your hair down before." He commented.

"Oh?" replied Crystal.

"Yeah it looks good on you." The dragon said awkwardly. This comment however, made Crystal blush and giggle to herself. The dragon then noticed that there was a little bit of worry in Crystal's eyes.

"Is everything okay?" he asked.

"Yeah..." sighed Crystal. "I'm just worried about my family in the hands of the Ministry. Especially my younger siblings."

"I can understand. You must be very worried." the dragon sympathized.

"I'm the eldest sibling in my family, and the eldest sibling does one of two things to their younger siblings," explained Crystal.

"What?" asked the dragon.

"They either torment them or protect them." she explained.

"Which one do you do?" asked the dragon.

"I do both." chuckled Crystal.

They both smiled and looked into each other's eyes. The dragon could see her worry welling up inside of her. He then leaned his head forward into the balcony.

"Obviously, at this moment, 1 can't physically give you a hug, but you can lean on me to take some of the strain off, and you can talk to me anytime because I'll always be listening." explained the dragon.

Crystal teared up and wrapped her arms around as much of the dragon as possible. Her tears came out slowly, first rolling down her skin then rolling down the dragon's scales. Eventually they both pulled away from each other.

"1 should uh…., get to bed." Stammered the dragon. He was not use to close affectionate contact with anyone. Be they human or be they some other creature. "Goodnight Crystal." he smiled awkwardly flashing his sharp teeth.

"Goodnight…" Crystal trailed off. "Goodnight, Richard."

"Wait, what?" the dragon asked.

"That's your name, Richard." She smiled.

"1 like it." The dragon smiled. He then took one last look at Crystal for the night and turned to go to his room.

When the dragon, his new name Richard got to his room, he fell asleep with Crystal on his mind.

Down at the pub sat a man. The man wore a jet-black suit while wearing a matching bowler hat. Standing up from his table revealed his long snake like stature. In long smooth strides he walked up the stairs that led to the rooms. He approached Crystal's room. He began to open the door. The man saw that Crystal was asleep in her bed. Making quiet steps to her bed, he came closer and closer. He now stood over top of her, slowly moving his cold icy hand to her forehead. Crystal's eyes suddenly jolted open to see the blurry darkened silhouette of the black suited man. She launched her fist at him, which knocked him to the ground. Crystal quickly put on her glasses to see what exactly she had hit.

"Well, you're a fighter." the man said, wiping a small amount of drawn blood from his lip. "1 like a challenge." he grinned.

"He-!" Crystal tried to cry for help, but the suited man had quickly rushed to grab Crystal by the throat.

Crystal started choking, as his icy hand pressed harder and harder against her throat, crushing her windpipe.

"I was wrong," the man chuckled. "This will be easy."

His long body then began to dissolve into a black dust like substance. The dust began to force its way into every opening of her face. Soon there was nothing left of the man. Sitting on the bed was just Crystal. She forcefully knocked off her glasses, revealing her face to have a dead look. She changed back into her clothes and walked out of her room with the same smooth, long strides as the man in the black suit.

To Be Continued...

Margaret and Joan's Moderately Neato Adventure

Throughout the late afternoon and early evening, Margaret and Joan prepared to go find Crystal.

"Do we have all that we need?" asked Joan.

"Hmmm... let's see, Mrs. Markle from next door will be taking care of the children... We have rope, medieval medicine, weaponry, and my carrot cake recipe." Margaret said, running a checklist.

"Mom, why do we need a carrot cake recipe?"

"You never know when we or someone else might want a good ol' fashioned carrot cake." replied Margaret, as she placed it ever so carefully into Joan's backpack.

"Very well." sighed Joan. "We should head out before the sun rises so the guards won't see us."

Once they had checked and double checked their checklist and had made sure that Mrs. Markle was watching the children, Margaret and Joan cautiously snuck out of their house. They crept quietly through the now empty marketplace. It was night, so the marketplace was quiet. So quiet that they could hear their own foot falls on the brick pathway. It seemed like clear sailing until they heard a foot fall that wasn't their own. Then suddenly, they heard several more foot falls.

"It's the guards." Joan whispered.

They started to run as quietly as they could away from the guards, attempting to disappear into the darkness. However, the guards began to catch up to them. Margaret then dashed into one of the old abandoned buildings.

"Joan, in here." she called.

Joan then followed close behind her, as they waited for the guards to pass.

"Phewww, that was close." Margaret said as she tried to steady her breath.

"Yeah, that was close." said a voice from behind.

Joan and Margaret both looked at each other and then turned around to face behind them. They almost had heart attacks, until they realized it was just Merlin. He was all locked up in shackles. He looked weak and beaten. However, what was most concerning about his appearance was he looked powerless and without magic.

"Merlin? What are you doing here all locked up?" asked Joan.

"Nothing is as it seems Joan." Merlin mumbled. "Their time is near..."

"Okay Merlin, please spare us the plot propelling obscurities, and just tell us what's going on." demanded Margaret.

"Nothing is real. We were all kidnapped by the Ministry, because we didn't have the Ball of Wisdom." explained Merlin. "We were all put under a spell. Bad things are upon us all. Joan, you need to find your daughter."

"Where and how do we escape?" asked Margaret.

"The east wall." Merlin said. "There's a hole you can get through."

"Mom, help me get these chains off Merlin." Joan said examining the chains for a weak spot.

"No." Protested Merlin. "Go on without me. If the Ministry finds out that I'm gone, people in the kingdom will suffer, especially your children. As of now Anthony, Hugh, and Wyllo are safe, along with the rest of the kingdom."

"He's right Joan." agreed Margaret.

Suddenly they all began to hear the footsteps of approaching guards. Like Thelma and Louise, Margaret and Joan took off, with the guards of The Ministry hot on their heels.

"Go. Hurry, and find Crystal." ordered Merlin his voice fading into the distance.

They reached the East wall, and while the hole was a tight squeeze they managed to get through. Once they were outside, they realized it was extremely cold, as they were surrounded on all sides by a frozen forest. A forest which was vastly unfamiliar to them and not the forest they knew that surrounded their kingdom.

"What are we going to use to get out of here?" asked Joan.

Margaret looked around quickly as she heard the guards shouting orders to capture them. Then she saw the very thing that could get them out of there in a hurry, a conveniently placed winged unicorn.

"Over there." Margaret pointed. "Ditch the license plates, and let's get out of here."

Margaret and Joan took flight in the unicorn. Its beautiful wings shone in the moonlight. If you dear reader wish it to be, visualize an E.T. reference. The guards stopped themselves short of the wall, as they watched Margaret and Joan escape the castle. Sandi, the leader of the Ministry, then materialized out of nowhere. Fear was struck in the hearts of the guards as she walked with intimidation to the edge of the wall.

"A thousand curses." She said with anger. "How could you let them escape???"

The guards began to quiver in fear of what Sandi could do to them. As the guards began to accept the possible thousand different fates that would curse them, Sandi then composed herself into a calm state.

"No matter." she stated. "The Ball of Wisdom and the Closet of Knowledge soon will be mine. Once I have those, all will be mine."

"Shall I send out demons to find them?" asked one of the guards.

"No." replied Sandi. "Since Mrs. Markle has had an unfortunate accident with her ankle and some stairs, someone will have to take care of the children. That someone will namely be me. They will be back, and we'll be waiting."

Sandi slinked silently toward their house. Meanwhile Anthony, Hugh, and Wyllo sat inside their house quietly, as their mother had instructed them. The time, however, that it was taking Mrs. Markle to arrive was making them all extremely bored. Mrs. Markle, having had her unfortunate accident, of course would not be coming. Hugh then turned to his siblings.

"Anybody else hungry or is it just me?" he asked.

Both Anthony and Wyllo nodded their heads simultaneously. With that the three of them hopped off their couch and into the kitchen.

"I am going to cook something amazing for us." Proclaimed Hugh confidently.

"What?" asked Wyllo.

"Eggs Benedict a la Hugh." He grinned.

Hugh then grabbed the step ladder and began climbing up to the cupboards.

"Hugh… do you even know how to cook?" questioned Anthony.

"Of course. Now I'm going to need some eggs, lots of eggs."

Anthony rushed to the cooler to grab several dozen eggs, while Hugh opened the cupboards revealing a dazzling array of sweets and candies. Dazzling mind you, if you're a ten-year-old and not diabetic.

"Wyllo! Catch!" cried Hugh as he threw down a cookie jar full to the brim with cookies, which Wyllo caught with precision.

"Let's see here." Hugh thought to himself. "Chocolate chips, jellybeans, pudding, marshmallows, baking powder, this will be awesome."

Hugh climbed down the ladder with all his ingredients and threw them all on the counter.

"Hugh, I got the eggs!" cried Anthony.

"Excellent." Grinned Hugh, tapping his fingers together devilishly. "Now the fun begins."

In a bowl Hugh combined 2 heaping cups of jellybeans, with 5 eggs. The colourful jellybeans contrasted terribly with the fresh yellow eggs, as he attempted to crack each egg with one hand. As you may have guessed, this resulted in many bits of eggshell in the mixture.

"I hope you two like crunchy eggs." He shrugged. "Now a little bit of pudding for colour."

Hugh then added a full cup of baking powder to the mix, along with a half cup of chocolate chips and a half cup of marshmallows. While Hugh mixed the ingredients together into a strange liquid mess, Wyllo quickly rushed over to the counter with a casserole dish. Hugh poured in the... the... what in the world do you call it again?

"Eggs benedict a la Hugh!" they shouted together.

Thank you. Hugh poured in the Eggs benedict a la Hugh... Ick... and Wyllo rushed the mixture to the cookstove. Then she placed it carefully in the section of the cookstove specifically designated for baking. The cookstove burned bright red with heat.

"Hugh?" inquired Anthony. "What are the cookies for?"

"Nothing really." Replied Hugh. "I just wanted cookies."

They each put a hand in the jar pulling out a handful of cookies. Each of them stared at the cookstove, their eyes filled with anticipation. Suddenly within three and a quarter minutes of baking, Hugh's creation began bubbling over in the cookstove. It began to rise uncontrollably, as the eggs and jellybeans began to burn. The smell of burnt sugar reached Anthony's nose.

"Fire!" he screamed in panic.

Black smoke suddenly came pouring out of the cookstove.

"What do I do?!?" panicked Hugh.

"I don't know!" replied Anthony. "You're the chef!"

"Water!" cried Wyllo.

Hugh rushed to the back of the house, grabbing a bucket of water, that had been there for just such an emergency. Flames were now visible as he rushed through the house spilling most of the water. Meanwhile Anthony was running around in circles in panic, grabbing all his toys, ready to evacuate. Wyllo concentrated on saving the cookies. However, Hugh arrived at the stove with the bucket of water. Splashing the water on the stove, it sizzled loudly, but put the fire out, and ruining the... Ick meal. Suddenly in walked Sandi, and another demon in human form.

"My oh my, look at all the chaos." She commented sweetly.

"Oh, Hugh you are so in trouble when mom gets home." Anthony snickered.

"Shut up Anthony..." mumbled Hugh.

"Now, now, there is no need for conflict." Assured Sandi. "Your mom has left me, Sandi the glorious head of the Ministry, to take care of you." She waved her hands in the air dramatically.

"Where is mom?" asked Anthony.

"Oh, don't worry, it won't matter." Piped up the demon from behind Sandi. "Because you'll never see your mother again anyways."

Anthony began to tear up slightly.

"Larry, can I see you for a minute in private?" asked Sandi as she gestured to the living room.

They both walked into the living room, shutting a door behind them.

"Larry, you're a good demon, who listens to orders." Praised Sandi.

"Thank you, ma'am." Larry beamed with pride. "I take my work as a demon seriously and obey all orders of my superiors to the best of my abilities plus 110%."

"Good. Now here's an order for you, button your lip!"

"Yes ma'am." Larry saluted sharply. "But I have to ask, do you happen to have a needle and thread so I can perform said task?"

Sandi slapped her forehead with the palm of her hand.

"It's an expression!" she cried furiously.

"My apologies."

"Listen, these children are much more than a hostage negotiation for the ball of wisdom." Explained Sandi. "My plan for them goes far beyond anything to do with the ball of wisdom. To deal with these children requires an intricate web of deception and false trust."

"I understand."

"Good."

Sandi then opened the door to the children in the next room.

"Don't worry children, your mom will be back soon. Larry here is just... not very bright." Smiled Sandi.

"Hey!" exclaimed Larry,

"Now, now, Larry, lip buttoned." Smiled Sandi,

"Yes ma'am…" mumbled Larry,

"Now children, why don't you three go play in the yard on the jungle gym?"

"But we don't have a jungle gym…" explained Hugh,

Sandi snapped her fingers,

"You do now." She smiled,

In the yard a jungle gym magically appeared. It had tons of swing ropes and twists and turns,

"Now, go play children." She waved creepily,

Anthony, Hugh, and Wyllo ran outside to play, while Sandi stayed behind and watched, grinning maniacally, hatching her mad plot,

I wanted to spoof Frasier, and I needed a story Segway. A match made in heaven,

"Joan, would you stop obsessively trying to clean our flying unicorn." Margaret said with a hint of a pompous British accent. "The author seems to want a satirical section of the story, spoofing Frasier."

"I know that, but do you realize how many small bugs carrying diseases are on this beast?" Joan spoke with an unquestionable tone of neurosis, of which could only be matched by David Hyde Pierce. "Besides, isn't this type of writing a sign of a lingering category DSM6 Hartley group therapy bed wetting disorder?"

All right that's Enough of That

A full night had passed as Margaret and Joan continued to search for Crystal on their flying unicorn. They were still a bit shaken up after finding out that they and friends and family were put under a spell, and kidnapped to a false reproduction of their own kingdom,

"Mom, I don't know what's more believable. Us searching for my daughter in far off lands on a flying unicorn, after escaping a twisted spell, or us doing really bad impressions of Kelsey Grammer and David Hyde Pierce." questioned Joan.

"I didn't write this." Margaret shrugged, as she continued to guide the unicorn.

A few moments of silence passed. The ground below began to turn slowly from cold snowy lands to warm green grasslands.

"What exactly is our plan?" asked Joan.

"I don't know." Margaret replied. "It's not every day that you're kidnapped with your entire kingdom and family."

"Is it safe to assume that Crystal wasn't kidnapped and is out there somewhere?" wondered Joan.

"That may be why we have to find her, before The Ministry does." Margaret explained. "She might have found the ball of wisdom by now, hence our kidnapping. They want it for something, and they were most likely going to trade the people for the ball."

"Brilliant deduction." Joan said. "However, I have one question."

"What?" Margaret replied.

"Why is the sky turning red in front of us?"

Sure enough, the sky was turning blood red all around them as complete shock came across both their faces.

"Mom, look out!" Joan screamed. They were headed straight for a massive murder of crows, that engulfed the horizon. There seemed to be no clear way to get through it.

Margaret turned to Joan and gave her a warning that Joan treasures to this very day.

"Joan, hang onto your natural defecations. I'm going to try to get us out of this."

Margaret then ordered the unicorn to go faster.

"Mom, you can't play chicken with crows..." Joan warned.

Margaret however didn't pay any attention to Joan's warning. The murder of crows and the unicorn came closer and closer to each other, both increasing in speed. Finally, they collided with each other. The crows went into a rage and started pecking at the unicorn trying to throw it off. Margaret and Joan began swinging at the crows wildly but decisively. The crows began to give up and leave them alone, however the last crow that left stole Margaret's carrot cake recipe out of Joan's backpack.

"Mom, they got your carrot cake recipe." exclaimed Joan.

Margaret looked back to see that the crow almost seemed to be taunting her. The look of fear and shock on her face turned to one of determination, and vengeance.

"No one takes my recipes, especially the one for my carrot cake."

Margaret immediately turned the unicorn on a dime and began to chase the crow. The crow led them in circles, loop de loops, and any other geometrical shape that can be drawn in the air. It is a well-known scientific fact that there are many different shades of the colour green. Joan was all of them.

"Mom, let him take the recipe, it's just carrot cake." protested Joan.

Margaret payed no attention to Joan. After a while of wild goose chases... sorry I mean wild crow chases, the crow finally began to slow down. Margaret flew the unicorn up close and attempted to grab the recipe. The crow flapped wildly, almost knocking Margaret to the ground. Margaret had quite enough of the bird, and swung her fist at it, hitting him dead in the throat. The crow plummeted to earth as Margaret plucked the recipe from its beak.

"Hahaha!" she cheered. "I got it!"

"Mom..." Joan said.

"Yes dear." Margaret replied looking at Joan's green colour coded face.

"That tree is getting very close to us." pointed Joan.

"So it is." surmised Margaret. "Joan you might want to hang on, it's going to be a rough landing."

I'm going to spare you the painful details of how the landing turned out. However, they are still alive, and yes, the unicorn is alive too.

"That is it mom." Joan said while trying to straighten her back while sitting in the tree. "Next time, I'm driving."

"Yeah..." Margaret groaned. "That would probably be the best ideaaaaaaahhh!"

Margaret had slipped off a tree branch and plummeted to earth.

"Mom, are you okay?" Joan shouted as she looked for her mother on the ground. She then found her lying flat by the base of the tree.

"I'm okay, just a pulled muscle here and there." Margaret said putting her thumbs up. "At least I saved the carrot cake recipe." She began waving it in the air for Joan to see.

Joan just sighed and eventually made her way down to the ground with the unicorn.

"You good, mom?" she asked.

"I'll be fine." replied Margaret as Joan helped her to her feet.

"What was with all those crows?" asked Joan.

"We either entered a really old horror movie, or it has something to do with the sky." Margaret replied gesturing to the blood red sky.

It was at that moment they both realized that they were now in the middle of nowhere. As they looked around to try and determine where they were, they were able to spot a small farm several hundred feet away.

"There might be someone in that farm over there that could help us." suggested Joan.

"What have we got to lose?" asked Margaret.

They both walked to the farm, making their way to the main house. The house was a small typical vine covered cottage.

"What? No white picket fences?" questioned Joan.

It so happened that at this cottage the fence was made from bright blue coloured pallets. As they approached the door, both looked around for any possible dangers. Joan knocked on the eggshell white coloured door. A few moments passed by, until suddenly there was an answer.

"Just a minute!" a woman's voice shouted. "I'm not decent yet!"

Eventually the door swung open revealing a petite woman that had wings on her back. She wore a white robe that almost seemed to not fit properly on herself.

"Oh, Sean, he's just a guy... just a platonic guy friend..." *Sigh

"Hi there." She greeted cheerfully. "My name is Mary Ann, who are you?"

"Well I'm Joan."

"And I'm her mother Margaret."

They each greeted introducing themselves.

Mary Ann smiled. "Come inside."

Margaret and Joan cautiously went inside, as they were still unaware if she was someone who could be trusted. The inside of the house was about as quaint as the outside. A few books here and there. The previous issues of Fairies Monthly magazines fanned out on a dark oak coffee table situated in the center of the living room.

"I don't get many visitors, what brings you here?" asked Mary Ann.

"We're looking for my daughter." explained Joan. "Her name is Crystal, wears glasses, about yea tall, a bunch of dark hair."

Mary Ann thought for a moment if she had seen anybody who even remotely looked like Crystal. All she could recall were the trolls she had traded spices within the days previous.

"I can't say I've seen anybody with that description." she sighed. "I'll definitely give you a hand to find her though."

"Thank you." thanked Joan.

"Do you know anything about the blood red sky out there?" Margaret gestured pointing out the window.

"I've actually been trying to figure it out myself." explained Mary Ann. "I think it has something to do with the Ministry."

"We actually came from the Ministry's headquarters..." stated Margaret.

Mary Ann seemed surprised. She knew that the Ministry had a reputation for apprehending people and never releasing them.

"You did?" she asked.

"Our entire kingdom was kidnapped and while we didn't know it at the time, we were under a spell that made us think we were at our own kingdom." explained Joan.

"We escaped, because we wanted to find Crystal." added Margaret. "After our escape we determined we were being held hostage until they could exchange us for the Ball of Wisdom."

"Wait a minute..." Mary Ann had a moment of realization. "It makes sense now."

She then started searching through the Fairies Monthly magazines. After determining the issue she needed, she began flipping through it vigorously searching for a specific page.

"Ah, here it is!" exclaimed Mary Ann. She snapped her fingers magically conjuring a standard number four, ballpoint, beige coloured, pen with blue ink. We can't be magical and sparkly all the time...

"Let's see here... This short and simple test will determine if a powerful force of magic which is supposed to be used for good has fallen into the metaphorical hands of evil." Mary Ann explained reading aloud from the magazine.

"All right. Has a magical item containing great power been stolen, such as a, ring, magical orb, or a D20 dye?... Check... Did someone randomly show up on your doorstep claiming to have escaped an evil organization?"

Mary Ann looked at Margaret and Joan for a moment.

"Check... Next question. Are there children in danger?"

"Quadruple check!" interrupted Joan.

"Ahem. Check. Do any of the children have a lightning bolt shaped scar?"

"No, definitely not." Answered Joan.

"Has there been odd fan-fiction written?" Mary Ann tapped the pen on her chin, thinking for a moment. "I'm just going to write down... Not yet... Final question... Is the sky red?..." She quickly looked out her window. "Quadruple check."

She took her pen and scribbled on the magazine page adding all the questions together.

"The answer is, yes. The Ministry now has the Ball Of Wisdom."

"What do we do?" asked Joan.

"Well first we have to... have to... have to..." Mary Ann was suddenly on the verge of sneezing. "Achoo!!"

Mary Ann had disappeared into thin air without any trace of her whereabouts.

"Ummm... Mary Ann?" Margaret called out.

Soon after Mary Ann's disappearance, she reappeared. Her cheeks were red as roses from apparent self-humiliation.

"Oh my gosh, that was embarrassing, I really have to learn to control myself." panicked Mary Ann.

"Chickie, are you okay?" asked Margaret.

"Yeah, you okay?" added Joan.

"Oh yeah, I'm fine." replied Mary Ann. "That's just a thing that happens when I sneeze. I get transported to wherever."

"Interesting." Joan commented.

"Yeah, did you know there are two whole other continents on earth?"

Before they could comment, Mary Ann began to get, what can only be described as, some sort of phone call via long distance magic.

"Oh no, Seán is calling me. Oh no, no, no, not after I embarrassed myself in front of him."

"Who is Seán?" asked Joan.

"Seán is... he's just a guy... you know your everyday run of the mill leprechaun who wanted something out of life and just magically strolled into my life one day." Mary Ann blushed. "You know, he's just a very platonic guy friend of mine."

"And you like him, more than a friend, right?" smiled Margaret.

"Maybe." Mary Ann replied trying to work up the nerve to answer the call. She was just about to answer when suddenly Margaret stopped her.

"Wait!" she cried.

What is it?" asked Mary Ann.

"You've got a couple of hairs out of place. You're already in a bathrobe, you at least want to look a little presentable for him." Margaret winked. That was the interesting thing about Margaret. Four grandchildren had given her the gift of a very natural Grandmother instinct. Whether it was her own Grandchildren that needed help, or someone else in need, Margaret would be there with her caring attitude.

Once Margaret had quickly fixed Mary Ann's hair, so it wasn't drooping over her eyes, Mary Ann answered the call and tried not to look like she had been panicking about her sudden appearance to Seán. A view screen appeared with Seán's face. Mary Ann couldn't help but blush a little bit.

"Oh, hey Seán, sorry about that sudden appearance. I didn't mean to, not that I didn't want to see you I just didn't want to visit you at that particular moment in time." she explained awkwardly.

"It's all right Mary Ann. I've actually called you to talk about the blood red sky." explained Seán. "You see there was this girl named Crystal, who had the Ball of Wisdom, and long story short she's been kidnapped with the Ball of Wisdom and the Closet of Knowledge."

Mary Ann's mind suddenly clicked when she heard the name Crystal. "Wait a girl named Crystal? Wears glasses? About yea tall? A bunch of dark hair?"

"Yes, that's her." answered Seán. "How did you know?"

Margaret and Joan's attention suddenly perked up. They gently pushed Mary Ann off to the side taking control of the conversation.

"Hi, I'm Margaret, I'm her grandmother."

"And I'm Joan, I'm her mother."

"Ah yes, Crystal has told me a little bit about you two on our trip to Moscow." Seán then looked to Margaret. "I've heard you have a fantastic carrot cake recipe."

"Well, I don't like to brag-"

"She went to Moscow!!!" interrupted Joan.

"Please ma'am, it's been a long story." pleaded Seán. "The bottom line is that Crystal has been kidnapped, and the fate of all civilized life as we know may rest in our hands."

Mary Ann pushed Margaret and Joan aside regaining control of the conversation.

"What do you need Seán?" she asked.

"I know that you live close to the unknown, if you can at least meet us at the edge of the known world, then we can go from there." explained Seán.

"Seán, it might be a good idea to bring Margaret and Joan." suggested Mary Ann. "They said they escaped the Ministry's castle, maybe they could lead us back to the exact location."

"Good thinking there Mary Ann, bring them along. We'll meet you at the edge of the known world, just look for the flying dragon who talks in fluent English."

"Wait, flying dragon? What are you talking about?"

"Like I said it's been a long story. Seán, signing off."

Seán hung up without giving any explanation to Mary Ann about the dragon.

"Margaret, Joan, do you think you can remember the way back to the Ministry's castle?" asked Mary Ann.

"I believe so." nodded Margaret.

"If they so much as harm one hair on my daughter's or any of my other kid's heads, so help me." proclaimed Joan angrily.

"Then I would say there is no time to waste." Stated Mary Ann. "Follow me, I've got the perfect transportation."

To Be Continued in Part Six...

Part Five

Sometime Earlier...

1t was early morning. The dragon... ah, 1 mean Richard awoke to the sound of wailing bagpipes, that seemed to be crying out like an emergency siren. Seán then suddenly burst into the room.

"Oh, mother of Mary, we've got a serious problem." he panicked.

"What's wrong?" asked Richard.

"Sir Nectarine was found unconscious. Crystal, The Ball of wisdom, and the Closet of Knowledge, all gone!"

"How can that be?" asked Richard. He then looked out the window and saw that the sky had turned blood red in colour. "Uh... Seán, the sky has turned blood red."

"Oh, dear 1 know. It seems The Ministry has taken everything they need. That's why I've got Michael sounding the emergency bagpipe alarm." explained Seán. "Come with me down to the pub."

Seán and Richard quickly rushed to the pub. The sky was blood red as far as the eye could see. Richard looked straight up and saw a murder of crows flying east, all making a terrifying noise that echoed through the land.

"Wait out here, I'm going to try and find Michael." Instructed Seán, when they arrived at the front entrance of the pub.

Seán entered the pub to find that everyone was in complete panic. Everyone was boarding up the windows and barricading any entrances, putting the pub into lockdown.

"THE END IS NEAR!!!" a voice screamed, which only added to the fuel of panic.

The panic was too much for Seán to bear. "Everyone BLOODY WELL CALM DOWN!!!" he screamed.

Seán was so loud that it shook the pub, and silence masked the panic.

"I know everything looks bad right now, but if any of us is going to figure this out, we need to keep a cool head, or we'll never beat the evil damnation that has befallen the land... Oh, that's just great... I sound like my father." Seán took in a deep breath to relax. "Now then, where is Michael?"

"Ack, right here cousin." Michael emerged from the hall where the Closet of Knowledge once was. "I've been trying to figure out what happened, and it's not good."

"What is it?" asked Seán.

As Michael and Seán went outside everyone continued locking down the pub, but in a more quiet and orderly manner.

"Ack, so you're the dragon I've heard about." Michael said to Richard.

"I've heard a little bit about you too. My name is Richard."

"You have a name?" questioned Seán.

"Of course, Crystal gave it to me last night." he smiled.

"I like it." Seán complimented.

"It's also a pleasure to meet you, lad. I only wish it were under better circumstances." smiled Michael awkwardly.

"The feeling is mutual." nodded Richard. "Now that introductions are aside, what in the world happened to the world while I was asleep?"

"Well, first there's the Closet of Knowledge, and the Ball Of Wisdom..." explained Michael. "There's nothing left in there, and no trace of where they took it to. All that was left was an unconscious Sir Nectarine."

"Last night, Michael and I suddenly fell unconscious last night, and when we woke up, everything was like this." explained Seán.

"Do you two remember anything?" asked Richard.

"All I can remember was that Crystal came down saying she couldn't sleep, and she wanted to hang out in the Closet of Knowledge." explained Michael. "There was that, but also a strange man running around the place lookin' for someone named Dean, but he left long before Crystal showed up. It was much later and after Crystal went into the Closet of Knowledge, that's when everything went black for me."

"Michael, did you happen to notice that Crystal had a bit of an odd look about her?" asked Seán.

"Now that you mention it lad, she did look strange." recalled Michael. "Sort of a dead look, like she wasn't there."

Seán turned his head to face his cousin more seriously.

"Michael, we could be lookin' at a case of possession."

"What are you talking about?" asked Richard. "She seemed fine before I went to my room last night."

"The Ministry once was a small powerless faction." explained Seán. "Unfortunately, nowadays their magic is powerful. They never used to be able to possess people, now it seems as if they can."

"I'm afraid lads that if we don't stop them, the world will be in for a terrible ride." Michael then looked up at the blood red sky. "The other problem is we don't even know where to begin to look for Crystal."

As they contemplated the issue, out of nowhere a woman in a white slightly oversized robe appeared right beside Seán.

"Oh, hey Seán." She smiled and waved awkwardly. "Soooo, how's it going?"

Seán seemed to know who the woman was, but before he could say anything in response she sneezed and disappeared into thin air.

"Who was that?" asked Richard.

"Ack, that was Mary Ann. Seán's sweetie." teased Michael.

"Michael, she is not my sweetie we're just good friends. Besides I think we have more pressing matters to take care of at the moment than turning this into an episode of Highland Hills 90210."

It was clear that Seán was irritated by Michael's comment.

"You're right lad, we have more important matters." agreed Michael.

"So, how are we going to find Crystal?" asked Richard.

Seán and Michael thought for a moment. They had no idea how they were going to find Crystal. Time was running short.

"You know." Seán said. "Mary Ann doesn't live that far off from the unknown, maybe she can get us into that area and help us find the Ministry's castle. I'll give her a call."

Seán spoke a few magical words, which caused a view screen to appear in front of him.

Michael then whispered something to Richard. "I told you that Seán liked her. He could've just followed the crows, because those birds go right to the source of evil. Instead he called Mary Ann. Also just look at that dumb grin on his face."

Richard then realized that Crystal had that same type of grin on her face the previous night when she gave him his name. Thinking of Crystal led Richard to think about how they had all arrived at this point in the first place. A feeling of guilt began to manifest itself in Richard, as he thought of his actions and felt that he had caused all this.

"I'm sensing a little bit of worry coming from you." commented Michael. "Wait strike that, a lot of worry."

"What are people going to say when this is over?" asked Richard quietly.

"What do you mean lad?" questioned Michael.

"What are they going to say about me?" explained Richard. "I stole the Ball of Wisdom, I caused this. The people of the kingdom, Crystal, her family, would all be fine right now. If I had just maybe said hello to a human, this wouldn't have happened... Now I may never be accepted."

"Lad, I know where you're coming from, but it's no use to cry over spilled milk at this point." Consoled Michael. "Besides there is no way to tell how anything in the past would've played out without you stealing the ball of wisdom. Things could be much worse as opposed to what they are now. Ack, like I said there is no way to tell."

"I guess you're right." Sighed Richard, as he let Michael's words sink in.

They soon saw Seán end his call with Mary Ann. He approached them confidently.

"Well boys, we're going' into the unknown. We just have to meet up with Mary Ann, and Crystal's Mother, and Grandmother." explained Seán.

"That's good lad, but if it's all the same to you I would like to stay and protect the pub." Michael said. "It's not that I don't have the highest confidence in the world that you'll be successful, but Sir Nectarine is still unconscious. Until he recovers, I need to protect this establishment and the people within it."

"It's okay cousin. We'll do our best." assured Seán.

Seán and Michael shared a brotherly hug. Michael then went over to Richard and gestured that he wanted to whisper something into his ear.

"Don't worry lad. Your friends will always be your friends regardless of anything, because that's what friends are."

Meanwhile at The Ministry's Castle...

Crystal, against her own will, was being forced into a darkened room of the castle. The man in the black suit had done his deed using Crystal's body. At this moment she is fighting from the inside attempting to regain control.

"I don't think I can keep her at bay much longer." The demon said, using its own voice but Crystal's body.

"You can leave her body now." Instructed Sandi. "She won't escape."

He worked his way out of Crystal's body. However instead of materializing into his creepy human form, he had materialized into his original demonic twisted form. Now fully removed from Crystal's body, he and Sandi watched from the shadows as Crystal slowly regained her own control. Crystal's eyes slowly blinked open. She stood up quickly.

"Who are you? Where am I?" demanded Crystal.

"Please dear child calm yourself. You're in the Ministry's care now. Please Sit down." Sandi said creepily.

"No, I will not sit down until you tell me where my family is!" protested Crystal.

"I SAID SIT DOWN!!!" Sandi shouted angrily.

The twisted demon then grabbed Crystal and threw her to the ground. Sandi then made herself visible to Crystal. She saw in Sandi, a sickly-sweet smile, but behind her eyes was a demonic presence.

"Now you see dear, if you cooperate with me, I will be nice." Explained Sandi. "Allow me to introduce myself, my name is Sandi."

Crystal couldn't help but snicker out loud.

"You dare make fun of my name?" questioned Sandi.

"Well I mean, you're a demon that runs an organization of demons determined to take over the world with unstoppable evil, and your name is just Sandi?" laughed Crystal.

Sandi was quite visibly furious at Crystal for laughing at her.

"Oh darn, I forgot you demons have sensitive egos." Crystal continued to taunt.

"ENOUGH!" Sandi's rage was so powerful that it was enough to shake the castle. Crystal's taunting smile then broke into a frown of fear. Sandi turned her back to Crystal and composed herself. She then turned back to look at Crystal with a smug evil look.

"Dear girl, you taunt me now, but your taunting is in vain. For I now have the Ball of Wisdom."

The twisted demon then threw the Ball of Wisdom like a large baseball to Sandi. She caught it in midair and began tossing it up and down into the air gleefully.

"You see, tonight at exactly seven minutes past midnight, we will be able to harness the power of The Ball of Wisdom with the power of the Closet of Knowledge. The combined power will give us a book, that will give me the power to rule overall." explained Sandi.

"Why seven minutes passed midnight?" asked Crystal.

"Think about it dear girl." Sandi said lightly caressing the ball with her long and fake fingernails. "Midnight is such a round and even number. For us 12:07 is perfect, for others it is an irritation, a perpetual torture for those who value their so called order. Ahahaahhahahahaha!" She laughed maniacally revealing her sharp yellow teeth. The twisted demon also joined in on the laughter.

"We will stop you!" cried Crystal.

"Oh, will you now." Sandi chuckled. "You, a little girl, an anti-social dragon, and a silly leprechaun who couldn't jig his way out of a wet paper bag, stop me?"

"Yeah, we're a strange crew, but being strange does not diminish what we can accomplish." replied Crystal.

Sandi snickered gleefully as she felt she had one more ace up her sleeve. She then conjured real time images on the Ball of Wisdom.

"Crystal, fates have already been sealed, just take a look at your siblings."

She then showed Crystal the Ball of Wisdom. Crystal saw her siblings all in the fake marketplace laughing and smiling like nothing was wrong. They were being entertained by a nanny type woman.

"Since your mother and grandmother made their untimely escape, I have had to take care or your siblings myself." Smiled Sandi maliciously. "I've actually grown to like them, and they've taken to our ways quite nicely."

Crystal didn't know what to say. The more she watched the more her own morality was crushed under Sandi's manipulative pressure. She almost felt a sense of betrayal by her siblings, as she watched helplessly as her siblings conformed to the ways of the Ministry.

"Take her to the dungeon." ordered Sandi.

The twisted demon grabbed Crystal's arm and began to drag her across the floor.

"Oh, Crystal dear." called Sandi. "In case you change your mind and decide that I am right, feel free to call me. I can always help you change your mind too, you know."

Crystal made a rude but appropriate hand gesture given the situation.

"Don't worry, young Crystal. For you are in a fragile state and I have a plan for you." Sandi thought to herself. Whatever her plan may be, it made her grin with a feeling of excitement.

The twisted demon dragged Crystal through the dark hallways. Lower and lower they traveled into the depths of the castle. A large rusty door swung open making a loud creaking noise that echoed through the darkness. Crystal tried to escape but was grabbed tightly and thrown into the cell. She lied on the floor completely still as the rusty door slammed shut. Her glasses had been knocked off her head.

Someone suddenly handed Crystal her glasses. Once she had put her glasses on, and her eyes adjusted to the darkness, she saw a girl about the same age as her standing overhead.

"Hi there, my name is Kelly," she introduced herself. "Welcome to the dungeon. At least it's not lonely down here anymore."

To Be Continued....

Part Six

Margaret, Joan, and Mary Ann stood at the front of a large barn. The barn was painted in wild psychedelic colours yet faded like a dreamy memory from yesteryear.

"All right chickie, what's this transportation you got for us?" asked Margaret.

"Wait and see." smiled Mary Ann.

She placed her hands together, then slowly parted them. As Mary Ann made this movement, the barn doors which were speckled with chips in the paint, slowly opened. Inside the barn was what appeared to be a World war one biplane.

"What... is that?" marveled Joan.

"It's called a biplane." answered Mary Ann.

"Where did you get such a contraption?" questioned Margaret.

"Well, I am a fairy with all powerful magic." explained Mary Ann. "Anyone with enough magic can time travel, past, present, or future. However, the council decided that it was too dangerous and banned time travel from being used. Except that I may have snapped up this beauty of flight minutes before the ban, or minutes after the ban, again time travel, who keeps track of time?"

"But why?" asked Joan. "To my knowledge all fairies can fly without anything mechanical."

"Joan, even us fairies and mythical creatures have our limitations." explained Mary Ann. She then stared lovingly at her plane. "With this plane I can soar above the heavens, and view a different perspective on life as I know it."

Margaret and Joan now eagerly approached the plane, while Mary Ann simply strolled over to her plane comfortably and began caressing the glossy outer hull. It was a true relic from the time it had come from.

"There's a lot of spells and magic in the world, but no spell is greater than the spell I get put under when I'm up there. Being able to kiss the sky, to fly across the open ocean. Nothing else except unlimited possibilities." she explained passionately.

Mary Ann then reached into a compartment in the cockpit grabbing a bright red wool scarf and her set of flying goggles. After placing the goggles on her head, she delicately wrapped the wool scarf around her neck, completing her pilot ensemble. Then she tossed Margaret and Joan each a pair of goggles. Margaret and Joan examined the goggles with a curiosity, as such a thing had never been conceived.

"Trust me you're going to need those." explained Mary Ann. "This baby goes a lot faster than any flying unicorn can. The airflow can be quite irritating to the eyes."

They put their goggles on and climbed into the plane, while Mary Ann stayed outside the plane.

"I'd say we're all about the same weight." She stated walking around the plane doing a quick pre-flight inspection.

"What do you mean?" asked Joan.

"Well it's just that with the center of gravity, and basic multiplication that if this plane is overloaded, it won't take off, we'll get in a tailspin and crash in a big fireball, but I think we should be fine."

"Wait what?" exclaimed Margaret.

Mary Ann didn't bother to answer Margaret. She went in front of the plane and spun the propeller by hand. After a few good spins the engine roared to life. Mary Ann jumped into the cock pit. Pulling the throttle slightly the engine received more power. Soon the plane began to drive out of the barn. Once out of the barn she guided it to a straight flat strip of land and gradually increased the speed. The ground below them passed by faster and faster. The flat strip of land was about to end. Before they hit the trees, Mary Ann pulled out the throttle and with a mighty burst of speed, the plane leaped off the ground into the air. When they reached a cruising altitude, Margaret and Joan looked all around the plane. They now understood what Mary Ann was talking about. Life looked vastly different from a height of a thousand feet. The rush Margaret and Joan experienced felt incredible as the world began to look small and insignificant. They felt as if they could conquer the highest mountain or tame the most savage beast.

"What did I tell you two?" Mary Ann asked rhetorically. "There are infinite possibilities up here. We could live, or we could die, but isn't the fear of death what makes life worth living?"

"You're an interesting character Mary Ann." Complimented Margaret. "We haven't even met half the characters in this story."

Ka-thunk, ka-thunk. Kelly was constantly bouncing a rubber ball against the dungeon wall to pass the time. This however was agitating Crystal. She was pacing back and forth and all around the dungeon cell, trying to figure a way out.

"Will you please stop that annoying bouncing, please?" pleaded Crystal.

"My Crystal, aren't we testy." teased Kelly.

"Gee, I don't know why." Crystal clearly had a sarcastic tone in her voice. "I went to go find the ball of wisdom for my kingdom, even though half the kingdom laughed at me and said I couldn't do it, because of my gender. Then I found out that said kingdom and my family was kidnapped by an evil organization composed of demons intent on taking over the world, so that's just very lovely. Oh, and now I'm in a dark dungeon imprisoned with a cell mate that won't stop bouncing a damned rubber ball."

Kelly didn't know what to say. All she could really say in response was that Crystal's rant would be a better recap of the story than anybody else's.

"Well, you know what they say. When life gives you lemons, pin them to the ground and beat the living tar out of them." Kelly then grinned widely. "How about we play a game?"

"A game, at a time like this? Are you kidding?" questioned Crystal. Crystal could only respond in a frustrated tone, as she began to question her cell mate's overall sanity.

"Now, now. We need to get our minds off our current situations." explained Kelly. "Now this game is my own invention, it's called Cleavers and Trolls."

"Cleavers and Trolls?" asked Crystal feeling somewhat curious.

"Yeah, it's a fantasy game, but it doesn't really require any pieces, or a board or cards. It can all be done in the mind. You can do anything and be anything. Imagination is your only required game piece." explained Kelly, as she made hand gestures to illustrate the majesty of her game.

"That's actually a pretty good concept, given where we are, and the lack of game pieces." Stated Crystal.

"Indeed, and now that you're here I can narrate certain scenarios and actions for you, instead of just narrating for myself."

"It sounds interesting, but I don't know..." debated Crystal.

"It's not like you're going anywhere. Trust me. I've looked for a way out and if there was one, I would be a figment of your imagination brought on by solitude right now." explained Kelly.

Crystal then raised an eyebrow of suspicion.

"How do I know you're not a demon trying to trap me into something?" she asked.

Kelly got up from her cot and went to the iron door.

"Yo, guard am I demon?" she shouted.

"humph." the guard groaned.

"No, you're not. You're just a really, really annoying human."

"Thank you, Ian, and remember keep smiling' away the day." teased Kelly. "Oh, that's Ian the guard by the way, he doesn't like me." Kelly explained to Crystal. "Now then what do you say, you want to give my game a whirl?"

Kelly now had so much excitement in her voice, it was difficult for Crystal to turn her down.

"I guess so." sighed Crystal.

"Perfect, this is going to be awesome." Kelly said excitedly. "Okay, okay, so your character name is Crystal. You have a bow and five arrows, and you're walking through the woods, when suddenly you see a man."

Crystal adjusted herself to a comfortable position, as she could tell this would be a long game. As they played, Crystal found there was something about Kelly that she could trust. There seemed to be some sort of mutual understanding of what they were both going in that cold, damp dungeon.

The sun was setting as Seán scanned the horizon looking for Mary Ann, while several degrees north east Mary Ann was looking for Seán in her biplane. Even though they were not together they both knew that time was running out.

"Where is this Mary Ann?" asked Richard.

"I don't know. They should be here." worried Seán.

They continued to circle the same area for a few moments. Suddenly Seán heard the distinct roar of an engine. Mary Ann seemed to come out of nowhere, as she pulled her plane up alongside Richard and Seán. She set her flying speed to match Richard's.

"Mary Ann is here to save the day boys!!" she shouted. "So, Seán, what's the plan?"

"First we find the Ministry, foil their plans, and save Crystal and the kingdom." explained Seán.

"Sounds like a good plan, but it has less detail than an undergraduate's thesis." replied Mary Ann.

"We're just going to have to make it up as we go along." smiled Seán.

Margaret and Joan then began to wave frantically to get Seán's attention.

"Hi, Seán" Margaret greeted. "We're your guides today."

"Excellent. This here is Richard." Seán introduced.

"Pleasure to meet all three of you." greeted Richard.

"Now then, since we seem to be all organized, it looks as if we don't have much time." Seán said pointing out the quickly setting sun.

"Right Seán." Mary Ann nodded. "Setting course for the unknown!" She shouted like a dork.

They all were concerned with the possible upcoming battles but now they were most concerned by the fact that nobody had brought sunglasses as the flew, squinted eyes into the sunset.

Meanwhile at Michael's pub...

"Ack lads, does everybody have their chanters tuned to their drones?" asked Michael to the group.

The Scotch on the Rock group all nodded holding their bagpipes in a ready to play position. Michael then stood in front of the band and began to give a short but inspirational speech.

"Now lads, 1 know there's already been a Braveheart reference in this story, but the Ministry is trying to take everything that we hold dear, but they will never take our, FREEDOM!"

Several members in the band raised their fists in agreement.

"We've got a long march ahead of us..." continued Michael. "However, lads, we will go the distance, because we are Scotch on the Rock. We will march through the hills of the Highlands, and through the driving snow of the unknown, because we are Scotch on the Rock. If our knees are about to freeze under our kilts we will continue to play, because we are Scotch on the Rock. If our reeds freeze up in the dead cold of the unknown, we will continue to play like never before because we are, SCOTCH ON THE ROCK!!!"

The band cheered wildly. Their adrenaline was to the limit.

"Now lads, FORM UP!" ordered Michael sternly.

While the band got in formation awaiting their next set of instructions, Michael walked quickly to the bar. At the bar was Sir Nectarine. He was conscious and had recovered nicely.

"Sir Nectarine, keep this pub safe with your life." Michael ordered.

"Yes sir." Sir Nectarine saluted. "It's a good thing the demon who possessed M'lady Crystal wasn't considering that I, a teddy bear, do not follow the basic laws of physics and magic, therefore I am able to recover quicker."

"Indeed it is lad." Nodded Michael.

Michael then noticed Sir Nectarine hanging his head low, seeming regretful.

"Ack lad, what's eating at your insides?" asked Michael.

"Sir, I must apologize for letting the Ministry steal everything and kidnapping Crystal. I should've been paying more attention." Sir Nectarine sighed in regret.

"Lad, the Ministry stealing the Ball of Wisdom and the Closet of Knowledge wasn't your fault." assured Michael speaking in a soft tone. "I'm glad you made a quick recovery, so I can go help Seán and his friends. Don't strain yourself though."

Sir Nectarine stared heroically into the distance.

"I won't let you down, sir." he said with confidence.

"Damn rights you won't." chuckled Michael. "Or you'll be drying sheep skin for the rest of your days."

They saluted each other one more time and Michael quickly marched his way to the head of the band. Michael made eye contact with the bass drummer, then with his feet counted out a quick march beat the band could play while marching.

"QUICK MARCH!" he shouted.

The band, in almost perfect formation, marched together in unison. Each began playing their bagpipes at the exact same time, making it sound like one loud bagpipe, blaring their tunes throughout the hills of the Scottish Highlands. The sweet snapping noise of the snare drummers and the deep melodic boom of bass drummer added flavour to the powerful tunes of the pipers. As they left the pub, the people could hear the tunes fade into the distance. The tunes of the pipers filled them with hope, but two questions remained. Would the band be needed, and if so, would they arrive in time?

Kelly and Crystal had quite a good time playing Cleavers and Trolls. Their laughter from the events of the game could be heard echoing through the dark dungeon hallways. It had been an unnecessary but much needed distraction.

"You know Kelly, this is a really fun game." complimented Crystal.

"Thank you." nodded Kelly.

"However, I think it needs a different name." suggested Crystal.

Kelly raised an eyebrow. "Oh?"

"Yeah, I don't know about the name Cleavers and Trolls. There were a bunch of dragons in it though, and you did create this game in a dungeon." explained Crystal.

Kelly tapped her finger on her chin contemplating a new name.

"Hmmmm... Dragons and Dungeons, Dragons... and Dungeons." she repeated to herself several times. "Nah. Sorry Crystal, I still like Cleavers and Trolls."

"It's all good. After all it's your game." Crystal smiled. She then stared at the door aimlessly.

"What's wrong?" asked Kelly.

Crystal sighed heavily. "Everything. I'm no closer to rescuing my family or the kingdom, and now the world is somewhat doomed."

Kelly could tell that the novelty of her game had worn off for Crystal.

"Chin up Crystal. We'll find a way out, or I'm not nuts." encouraged Kelly. "Trust me Crystal that's a bold claim for me to make, because well... I am."

Crystal admittedly had become a little scared by Kelly's statement.

"No, not nuts in the bad way." Kelly explained. "I'm nuts in a good way, like walnuts. High in protein and you can throw me on salad."

Crystal smiled and admired Kelly's confidence, knowing full well that Kelly had been in this dungeon herself for a long undetermined amount of time. Suddenly the large iron door opened and standing in the doorway was Joan. Crystal was visibly shocked to see her mother.

"Mom, you're okay?" asked Crystal.

"Of course, honey." replied Joan convincingly yet deceivingly.

Joan then walked up close to Crystal and sat next to her. She looked at Crystal, eye to eye.

"The Ministry are really nice people." She said bluntly.

"Nice?" Crystal questioned.

"Yes honey, they'll take care of us, they'll take care of the world." explained Joan. "Their rule is law."

The way Joan talked was hypnotic to Crystal, as Crystal nodded in agreement to almost everything she said.

"I can take you to your brothers and sister. We can be a family of the Ministry." smiled Joan eerily.

The adventure, so far, for Crystal had taken a toll on her overall mental strength. Her mind, weak and tired from everything that had happened, sought an easy solution in the words that Joan was telling her.

"I would like to see them again." She said.

"Crystal" interrupted Kelly. "Something isn't right..."

"Don't worry so much Kelly. This is my mom." assured Crystal.

"Yeah Kelly, don't worry so much." added Joan.

Joan then turned to Kelly and whispered in a low voice that Kelly could hear but Crystal couldn't.

"Or it's the rack for eternity for you."

Joan turned back to Crystal, showing Crystal her eerie but sweet smile.

"So Crystal, shall we go? They're all waiting."

Crystal thought for a moment or two, wondering only for a minute if this was fake. However, the thought of keeping her siblings safe by any means triumphed overall.

"Okay let's go, but can we bring Kelly?" She asked. "She's my new friend."

"Yeah, can we bring Kelly?" Kelly asked sarcastically, referring to herself in the third person. "Kelly wants to see how this turns out."

"What did I tell you?" Joan fumed gritting her teeth at Kelly. She then put on her smile again for Crystal.

"Of course, honey, we can bring Kelly."

They all stood up and walked out of the dungeon. Joan, however, made sure that Kelly stayed well behind herself and Crystal.

"We better hurry Crystal" Joan said. "There's not much time left."

"There's not much time left!" Seán shouted to Mary Ann, as he pointed out the position of the moon.

"Margaret, Joan, we need to find the Ministry's castle! Time is running out!" warned Mary Ann.

"It should be appearing any minute!" assured Joan.

Sure enough, the ground below turned from grass to snow. The air around them also became frigid and cold, as snow began to rush past them. The Ministry's castle came into view through the almost blizzard like snowfall. It was large and ominous, a form of chaotic order. All the crows that they had seen were now all swarming the castle in even bigger numbers.

"Seán, I won't be able to keep this plane in the air much longer with this snowstorm!" Mary Ann shouted. "I'm going to land a little way from the castle!"

"Sounds good Mary Ann, we're right behind you!" replied Seán.

Once landed, they all re-grouped themselves to figure out a plan.

"Okay what's the plan?" asked Margaret.

"Well the castle is surrounded by demon guards, so getting around them would be our first step." explained Seán.

Mary Ann suddenly got an idea. "If I remember correctly, a demon guard's biggest weakness is carrot cake."

They all turned slowly and began looking at Margaret. She then turned to face Joan.

"See, what did I tell you? You never know who's going to want a good ol' fashioned carrot cake recipe."

"Yes mom. You were right." laughed Joan. "Once this is all said and done, I'll catch one of those crows and eat it."

Margaret pulled out the recipe from her pocket.

"How do you expect me to make this?" she asked.

"Ah yes, there does seem to be a lack of cooking utensils." observed Seán.

"As well as a lack of time." added Margaret. "This takes time to make. You cannot rush something so complex and beautiful as carrot cake."

"Please give me the recipe, I can whip it up in no time." instructed Seán.

Margaret handed Seán the recipe. He looked it over and began using magic to create the carrot cake.

"Seán, you can cook?" asked Mary Ann.

"Yeah it's something I picked up." he replied. "My older cousin Maggie taught me."

"Oh, Seán you're wonderful." blushed Mary Ann. She began to literally drift up to the ninth cloud. Richard however grabbed her by the leg and pulled her back down to earth.

"Mary Ann, the plan, remember?" he said.

"Right, right." Mary Ann shook her head to snap herself back into reality. "Once Seán has the carrot cake made, Margaret and I will try to coax the guards into taking it. The rest of you will be hiding off to the side. Hopefully they won't be able to resist the cake. We'll sneak past the guards, then split up inside the castle to find Crystal, and foil the Ministry's plans. Any questions?"

"How are we all sneaking past the guards, exactly?" asked Margaret.

"Seán is putting a little extra ingredient in the carrot cake, that will put them to sleep." explained Mary Ann. "Speaking of which, I believe Seán is finished." She said smelling the air.

It was so cold that they could see the heat radiating from the cake. They now all understood why a demon would weaken to such a baked good. It smelled and looked irresistible.

"So, do we all understand the plan?" Mary Ann asked the group.

Everyone nodded confidently. Margaret and Mary Ann walked up to the entrance of the castle approaching two of the guards while everyone stayed back out of sight.

"Who goes there?" One of the guards asked fiercely.

"We're just a couple of traveling bakers." lied Mary Ann.

"Yes, we're trying to introduce the world to our style of baking." added Margaret.

"Move along! This is no place for." The guard stopped talking and began sniffing the air. "Is that carrot cake?" he asked.

"Why yes." replied Margaret. "It's a very special recipe."

The guard looked over to another guard.

"Joe, they've got carrot cake." he said.

"It does smell wonderful." replied Joe. "How much?"

"Consider it a free sample." smiled Mary Ann and she handed the cake to the guard.

Both guards took a piece of the steaming cake and gobbled the orange spongy delicacy down into their stomachs.

"This is amazing." commented Joe. "Hey everyone, come try this carrot cake. It's the best one I've ever eaten!" he called out to his fellow guards.

Suddenly, the one area had all the guards, eating the carrot cake. Margaret and Mary Ann watched with grinning smiles, as each guard, one by one, began to pass out and fall asleep. Once they were all completely asleep, Mary Ann gestured the group to come forward. They all tip toed past the sleeping demons, heading into the main hall of the castle.

"Wow, that actually worked." Commented Joan

"All right, this is where we all split up. Margaret and I will take care of finding and rescuing the kingdom's people. Seán and Joan, you find Crystal. Richard, try and find a means to stop the Ministry." explained Mary Ann. "I don't know how long those guards will be out for, so we need to work quickly."

They all split up going in different directions throughout the castle.

Joan, Crystal, and Kelly walked into a large room that was glowing with magic. Crystal could see, sitting on a bench with fluffy pillows, her siblings, Anthony, Hugh, and Wyllo.

"Hey sis, how's it going'?" Wyllo smiled.

"Fine, I guess." Replied Crystal.

"Crystal, the Ministry is so cool."

"Yeah Crystal, the Ministry gives us whatever we want, and it's awesome." explained Anthony.

"Is this true mom?" asked Crystal.

"Why of course honey." replied Joan. "Being a family of the Ministry is for the good of all of us."

Kelly had heard quite enough and decided to speak up.

"Crystal, does any of this sound right to you?" she asked. "That question is also rhetorical, because none of this seems right."

A demon then slinked up to Joan and whispered something.

"What is Kelly doing here?" he asked.

"Crystal wanted to bring her." She whispered back. "In order to keep this charade going I had to bring Kelly."

"Mom?" Crystal asked. "Is being with the Ministry good for the family?"

"Of course, it is honey." replied Joan. "It's good for everyone. Now let's all play a fun game, called ask for anything you want."

"Yayyy!!!" they all cheered, except Crystal. She simply nodded, completely unsure of everything that was happening in the moment. Joan pointed at Wyllo.

"Wyllo you get to go first."

"I want a pony and a makeup kit."

Joan snapped her fingers, and a large make up kit appeared in Wyllo's lap. A majestic pony also appeared behind her. The pony began licking Wyllo lightly, and she began laughing with joy. Joy however, that was composed from greed.

"Anthony, Hugh, it is your turn now." Pointed Joan.

"We want real weaponry, not that cheap plastic stuff." Anthony said speaking for both.

Joan snapped her fingers again, and real weaponry and armor appeared on Anthony and Hugh. Meanwhile the real Joan and Seán were watching out of sight from everyone.

"Why that imposter, she's spoiling my children." The real Joan fumed. "That is not how I raise my children. This is epic proportions of unicorn poop!"

"Easy now Joan, maybe we want to go at this with a cool head." suggested Seán. "This is what they do to gain false trust."

"Fine..." sighed the real Joan.

"We wait for our moment." Seán said.

The fake Joan turned to Crystal. "Now Crystal it's your turn, ask for anything you want."

Crystal looked at her siblings. She then looked into her fake mother's even faker eyes.

"I want my family." she said.

"But Crystal sweetie, this is your family."

"This isn't our family; this isn't who we are." Protested Crystal. "Giving us anything and everything we want??? While also conforming to an evil organization??? Are you flippin' crazy lady???"

"Couldn't have said it better myself." Nodded Kelly.

The fake Joan, in response, grabbed Crystal's arm harshly. "Are you talking back to me?" The fake Joan snarled angrily.

"Mom, you're hurting me."

The real Joan seeing all of this unfold had seen quite enough.

"This is moment enough for me Seán." she said.

Like a mother grizzly bear, the real Joan raced out into the open area bravely.

"Get your sickly-sweet impersonating dog hands off my daughter!" she demanded.

"Oh no Crystal, somebody must be trying to play a head game with you by getting one of their own demons to pose as me." lied the fake Joan. She lied badly I might add.

The real Joan now became completely furious.

"First you kidnap me, my family, my friends, my entire basic way of life. Then you try to earn MY children's love by bribing them, and now you're saying I'm not who I am??? I don't know who you think you are lady, and I don't give two fecal deposits of what you think of me. I have sacrificed everything for MY children, including my very, very weak bladder. Yeah, C-sections in the medieval times... NOT THAT GREAT. I will not have some evil demon lady who has never even had children, teach MY children how to be greedy and think magic will get them anything they want." The real Joan paused for a moment examining the fake Joan. "Also, I would NEVER wear those shoes with that outfit."

"You see Crystal, she's filling your head with inanimate nonsense." The fake Joan continued to lie while still holding onto Crystal tightly.

Crystal looked at both Joans. She looked deeply into her real mother's eyes, then looked deeply into her fake mother's eyes. Many things in life cannot be broken, and one of those things is the bond between parent and child. Crystal saw in her real mother's eyes every moment of joy that Crystal and her siblings had brought to her, as well as every moment of terror. In her fake mother's eyes, there was simply nothing. No, love, no joy, no terror. Crystal turned to the fake Joan.

"Let go of me." demanded Crystal.

"Dear sweet little Crystal, can't you see?"

"You heard me." Crystal said. "Get your sickly-sweet impersonating dog hands off me." She then forcefully pushed herself away from her imposter mother.

"That's my daughter who said that." beamed Joan with pride.

Crystal ran to Joan and embraced her in a hug. They held this hug for quite some time. Seán also made his presence known, as he walked into the open.

"Where in the world were you?" asked Joan.

"You seemed to have it pretty much covered with your whole motherly speech." Replied Seán. "Also, I can see Crystal definitely takes after your side of the family."

Joan and Crystal grinned together. While the fake Joan had transformed back into Sandi. Anthony, Hugh, and Wyllo, were all equally confused.

"So, wait a minute, this Sandi person was posing as mommy?" Wyllo pointed at Sandi. "And that's real mommy." She then pointed at Joan. "Sandi, that wasn't very nice to try and trick us."

"We got this cool stuff from you Sandi, but it was wrong to trick us." stated Anthony. "I want to be with our mom, our real mom."

Anthony admired his shiny metal armor, and sharpened sword.

"At least we get to keep all this cool stuff." He exclaimed gleefully.

Sandi hearing this, snapped her fingers. The Pony, the makeup kit, and the weaponry/armor all disappeared. Wyllo and Hugh glared at Anthony.

"GOOD WORK ANTHONY!!" they said together in furious sarcasm.

Joan, Crystal, Seán, and Kelly all shared a laugh.

"Enough of this." demanded Sandi. "It's too late for you now. You are my prisoners."

"Oh, are we now?" Seán questioned. "I'll tell you somethin', we're going to foil your plans, and get everyone out of here, and be back home in time for a midnight snack."

Seán then got into position to start his famous fighting Riverdance. However, Sandi looked at Seán bowing gracefully and laughed aloud.

"You're kidding me, right?" she asked sarcastically.

Sandi raised her hand, which shot out a magic blast that hit Seán and rendered him unconscious. The entire group was shocked, as they looked at Seán's body sprawled out on the floor. Sandi looked dead into Crystal's eyes.

"I told you he couldn't jig his way out of a wet paper bag." she giggled maniacally. "Apprehend all of them and lock them up in here. I want them to have a front row seat when our plans are completed."

The demons apprehended them all. The group struggled to get free, a futile move, as the demons were holding them in an unescapable grip.

"What about the others?" asked a demon.

"I've got an ambush waiting for Margaret and Mary Ann." explained Sandi. "I have what I need. So, I returned the people of the kingdom to their proper home. All they will find is my guards ready to capture them."

"And the dragon?" the demon asked.

"Don't worry, his own vulnerabilities will trap him." Sandi grinned. "Lock them up. It will be an exciting night."

Margaret and Mary Ann were confused. They had found the fake kingdom, but there was no one around. It was quiet, and dark, almost abandoned.

"Where is everyone?" asked Mary Ann.

"I don't know." worried Margaret.

Suddenly demons emerged from the shadows, attempting to snatch them.

"It's an ambush!" cried Mary Ann. "Run!"

Margaret and Mary Ann split up running for their lives. Margaret ran through the marketplace throwing large items onto the ground to try and create obstructions for the demons. Mary Ann also attempted to do the same thing as she ran through numerous houses. However, the way the reproduction was laid out, they both found they were both travelling in circles. Eventually they both ended up at the end of a dead-end alley.

"What do we do now?" panicked Margaret.

Mary Ann didn't know what to do. The demons surrounded the alley and closed in to capture them.

Richard walked through the dark hallways quietly and cautiously. He tried not to make noise, even though his size went against being quiet. He then came upon several cells. He investigated one and saw Crystal.

"Crystal!" Richard exclaimed. "I'm so glad I found you."

She looked to face Richard and gave him an irritated look.

"Well I'm not glad you found me." she replied.

"What are you talking about?" Richard asked being confused.

"What do you think? You stole the Ball of wisdom. It's all your fault!" Crystal had anger in her voice, as Richard began to feel hurt. "I can never be friends with you, and no human will EVER be friends with you!"

Richard was shocked as he took a step away from the cell. Her words cutting into him like a sharp sword. He turned his head away. Thinking carefully, he composed himself. After careful over analysis of the situation, he realized that this was not the Crystal he knew.

89

"No." he said. "You're not Crystal. The Crystal I know is... is... far more than you will ever be. Good day, Ma'am."

Richard then slowly walked away from the Crystal in the cell. She then gritted her teeth roughly.

"Attack!" she ordered, which echoed through the hallways.

Richard hearing this tried to make an escape, but the demons were too fast for him as they launched at him tackling Richard to the ground. He then saw out of the corner of his eye, the imposter Crystal transforming back into a demon. The demon knelt beside him.

"You caught on faster than most." she spoke ominously. "You must be more powerful than your vulnerabilities." She then locked Richard's mouth in a muzzle.

In the large room where the Ball of Wisdom and the Closet of Knowledge were being kept for the appointed hour, the demons paraded Margaret, Mary Ann, and Richard in front of Joan, Crystal, Seán, and Kelly, who were locked up in shackles. The demons then locked them up in shackles. There, the Ball of Wisdom and Closet of Knowledge sat in front of them. Sandi had indeed given them front row seats to their nefarious activities.

"Is everything ready?" Sandi asked one of the demons.

"Yes." he replied.

"Perfect." grinned Sandi. "I can see it's already happening."

Our heroes all watched helplessly as the Ball of Wisdom began extracting information from the Closet of Knowledge, which was a creating an all-powerful book of evil. The moon shined brightly through the windowed ceiling, bathing the process in a brilliant white light, which didn't really do anything, but it looks really cool.

"Sandi, it's midnight." a demon said in a rough old voice.

"Seven more minutes and the world shall be mine. Hahahahahahaha!" Sandi's laugh shook the room.

"I'm sorry everyone..." Sighed Crystal.

"Don't be sorry Crystal." Joan said. "So, the world is going to be under a bad ruler for a few years. Look at the adventure we all had, we made new friends, and strengthened ties with family."

"You're right mom." smiled Crystal.

Richard also nodded in agreement not being able to talk as he still was wearing the muzzle.

"It has been a great honour to meet and work with all of you." Seán beamed.

"Seán, there's something I want to tell you." Mary Ann blushed.

"Go on."

"Well it's that... it's that... it's just that..." Mary Ann stuttered slightly. "I-"

"Aggghhhhh! Enough!" cried Sandi feeling annoyed. "Good grief, and you people call me sickly sweet."

Kelly then spoke up angrily.

"Listen lady, you're going to rule the world in six minutes, which means we have six minutes of freedom of at least thought and talking left. So, shut up and let us all have our moment."

"Oh, dear girl, you will pay when I rule all..." Sandi fumed.

"Hey, what did I say? Mo-ment, our moment."

Sandi angerly gritted her teeth to keep herself quiet, but in her mind she plotted to exact her revenge on Kelly, which was the only thing preventing her from completely snapping from Kelly's rebelliousness.

"Thank you." nodded Seán. "Now, Mary Ann what were you going to say?"

Mary Ann looked away from Seán, feeling that the moment was gone. "It was nothing."

Seán shrugged in his shackles. They each stared at the clock, watching every second and minute pass by.

"Well... I guess this is it." stated Margaret, as the minute hand moved itself to the six-minute position.

They all looked at each other in silence. It was a long six minutes. Suddenly Crystal heard something strange break the silence.

"Is that bagpipes?" she asked.

Even though everyone could hear it too they ignored her, thinking they were just imagining it in order to give their minds a false hope. The sound of Bagpipes however got louder and louder. The sound of the now looming Pipe band had a strange effect on the demons as they began to Highland dance. Sandi however was not affected, just extremely irritated.

"What are you doing?" Asked Sandi, with a frustrated tone.

The demons were now too entranced by the tunes to take orders from their superior. The sound of bagpipes was now right on top of them, as Michael and his band suddenly burst through the wooden doors heroically, playing a jolly tune.

"Michael!" Seán cried. "You came to save us!"

The band's playing was powerful as they all entered the room in perfect formation. So powerful, that once the drummers started playing, the vibration was enough to magically unlock everyone's shackles. Once freed, Crystal, Margaret, and Joan looked each other in the eyes then looked at the ball of wisdom, knowing exactly what to do. They all smiled, putting their heels together, then bowing graciously to one another, they Highland danced their way to the ball of wisdom to put an end to the evil as the band played on. Sandi was now severely weakened by the band. She watched helplessly as Crystal danced around the ball of wisdom several times before gracefully plucking it from its pedestal of evil.

"Nooooo!!" Sandi screamed, as she tried to grab Crystal. However, Crystal tauntingly danced out of Sandi's reach. Kelly even decided to join in, as she danced on those that had kept her in the dungeon for so long.

The band beautifully ended their tune, and the demons became unconscious as there was nothing left with which to dance. The odd silence that normally occurs once bagpipes have finished playing immediately made itself known. Seán then walked up to Michael.

"Ack, sorry I'm late cousin." apologized Michael. "Aron's chanter just wouldn't get in tune with the rest of the band, had to get him a new reed and everything."

Seán just sternly stared at his cousin attempting to keep a straight face.

"You say that you're not going to be able to make it, and then somehow like a miracle you show up anyways. What kind of an Engineer Scott impression is that?" joked Seán.

"Ack, a pretty damned accurate Engineer Scott impression I'd say." laughed Michael. "Besides, would you rather see my Paul McGillion impression instead?"

"Oh no, please don't." Pleaded Seán. "Regardless Michael, we're all happy to see you and your band... well, some of us our happy."

Seán then looked at Sandi who was still plugging her ears, in pain and frustration. Crystal then came running up to Seán.

"Seán, I got the Ball of Wisdom." she said.

"Excellent." praised Seán. "Now we best get out of here."

"What about the Closet of Knowledge?" asked Crystal.

"We can always make a new one." replied Seán. "A ball of wisdom on the other hand is irreplaceable."

Sandi then began to regain her stamina, as well as the other demons. Sandi looked furious as her eyes turned blood red.

"GET THEM! GET THEM!" she ordered loudly.

"Ack cousin, you better get your group out of here." ordered Michael. "We'll try and hold the demons in here at bay."

"Michael, we can't leave you and the band here alone." protested Seán.

"Don't worry about us lad, we'll be fine." assured Michael.

"Fine, but your mother better not blame me for whatever happens to ya'."

Seán then ordered everyone to get out as fast as possible.

"Everyone get out of here together and this time we stick together."

Joan picked up Wyllo and carried her while Anthony and Hugh followed close behind. Once Michael could see them making their way out of the room, he gestured to the band to begin playing again.

"Lads, you know what to play." he smiled.

Once again, the band began playing. The tune was enough to weaken the demons, enabling our heroes to escape the room. Kelly led the way as they ran through the maze of dark hallways. The sound of Scotch on the Rock could still be faintly heard as the tunes echoed through the castle.

"Any idea where we're going?" asked Margaret.

"Yes, there should be some kind of way out, any moment now." explained Kelly. "It should just be around this corner."

They all rounded the corner to find that it was completely blocked off by demons, ready to attack.

"What do we do now?" asked Joan.

"Crystal, get everyone out of here to safety." instructed Richard. "I'm going to hold back the demons for as long as I can."

"I can't just leave you to take on all those demons." protested Crystal.

"No" argued Richard. "I'll be a distraction, at least you and everyone else can get to safety."

"Crystal, I don't think there's time to argue about this." advised Seán, as the demons drew closer.

"But..." Crystal sighed.

"No buts." Richard cried, as he charged into the demons head first. "Come on demons show me what you got, Ya wussies."

The demons charged at Richard. They clawed him and bit him. However, our hero fought relentlessly, until a hole of safety had opened to the outside. The rest of our heroes dashed outside to a safe vantage point.

"I need to go back in there and help Richard." exclaimed Crystal.

Suddenly the group noticed that the castle was beginning to shake.

"What's going on?" asked Crystal.

"It's Michael and his band. They're playing so loud that it's going to knock down the castle." explained Seán.

"I have to go back and get Richard out of there." Cried Crystal.

Before Crystal could run back to the castle, Seán grabbed her preventing her from moving.

"Crystal, you can't. It's not safe."

Crystal watched helplessly as she saw bricks of the castle crumble to the ground. Inside the castle, Richard could feel the shake as he continued to fight the demons. Michael and his band could also see that the room they were in was crumbling all around them. Scotch on the Rock stopped playing for a moment. Michael looked at his band and nodded. The band seemed to know what to play as they struck up their bagpipes and began playing Amazing Grace.

Sandi watched in horror as she realized her dream to rule the world had crumbled and her castle was about to do the same.

Outside the group saw that the castle was shaking even more violently. Suddenly they heard a large crash, as one of the taller towers fell to the ground. From there, a domino effect took place as the castle began to fall apart completely, until there was nothing left but rubble. An ominous silence filled the air, as the band or Richard couldn't be seen.

"Richard!" Crystal cried.

Seán lost his grip on Crystal. She ran down to the now destroyed castle. Everyone else followed close behind. They all began digging through the rubble trying to find any survivors. They had no luck. The castle lay completely in ruins, with no sounds of any kind, not even a call for help. Crystal was almost completely distraught. She then sat down in the rubble and began to cry. Margaret, Joan, and her siblings gave her a family hug. Seán sympathetically patted her on the back.

"I know, Scotch on the Rock, and Richard gave their lives for us..." stated Seán. "We'll never forget them."

Seán and everyone else bowed their head, in silence. All of a sudden in the silence they heard the sound of multiple sets of bagpipe drones striking up. Then they heard the beautiful but piercing sound of bagpipe chanters playing the catch note E. The rubble below them began to move, as the tune was played. They all stepped away. Out of the rubble emerged Michael as well as the rest of Scotch on the Rock, playing the last two lines of Scotland the Brave. The tune ended, and last but not least, but a little beaten up, Richard emerged. Crystal ran over and gave him a hug, to which Richard did his best to accommodate her and not make it awkward.

"Hahahaha." Michael laughed. "Lads, I'd like to see Mel Gibson top what we just did today."

They all laughed a well-deserved laugh. Their laughter however was cut short, as the ground began to shake. Emerging from the rubble was a dirty evil looking hand. The group rushed the children to Richard's protection. They all prepared to do battle as Crystal wielded a sword, Seán clicked his heels together, and Margaret held firm a stale rock-hard piece of carrot cake. The rubble suddenly parted. What emerged was terrifying, it was... it was...

"For Pete's sake! Has anyone seen Dean?!?!"

Epilogue

ere we are dear reader, the end of the story. I think I might cry, because the adventure is... is... over! Boo hoo, hoo! So much has happened, so many new friends. *Sniffle. Lionel please get me a tissue, and perhaps a pint of that ice cream that has a German sounding name but is actually made in New Jersey.

Pardon me... Now then, our heroes returned as... well heroes. Out of the bright morning sky flew the winged dragon Richard and the biplane of Mary Ann. Atop Richard was Crystal, holding the ball of wisdom firmly in her hands, making sure that it would never fall into the wrong hands again. The kingdom, seeing the strange crew flying just overhead, began to draw mass amounts of attention as the people began to gather in the marketplace. However, after seeing all the people gather, Richard became frightened.

"No, no, I can't land." He protested. "Many people, too many people..."

"Come on Richard." Encouraged Crystal.

"Waaayyy too many people. I'm not ready for this..."

"Richard." Crystal spoke sternly, but sweetly. "You took on multiple demons, you can handle a few people."

Richard's anxiety was mildly soothed by Crystal's voice, as he made his best attempt at confidently landing inside the kingdom. As he lowered himself down to the ground, the crowd moved to give him space. The people were all too confused by the events of the past few days to do or say anything.

"What?" Kelly asked comically. "You never saw a girl who just saved your behinds riding with a leprechaun and a former prisoner of the Ministry on a dragon with the rest of her family following close behind in a bi-plane before?"

"Actually Kelly…" whispered Seán. "They never have seen a bi-plane before…"

"Oh…" comprehended Kelly. "Well, neither have I to be honest. Hey that's something we all have in common." Kelly then leaned in close to Crystal. "Crystal, I think me and the people of your kingdom are going to become very good friends. I wonder if they'll like Cleavers and Trolls."

"Most likely." Smiled Crystal.

Crystal leapt off of Richard's back, when suddenly the crowd parted and out emerged King Alloicious.

"Would someone like to explain to me what in the world is going on?" he asked.

Crystal simply knelt down before King Allouicious presenting the ball of wisdom to him.

"Your majesty." She declared.

"Young lady." He replied. "I am now more confused than I was five seconds ago."

"Well you see, it be like this your Majesty." Piped up Seán.

"Wait a minute." interrupted King Alloicious, as he looked more closely at Seán's face. "You're the fellow who wouldn't give me three more wishes."

"I remember." Frowned Seán. "And I told you already, you can't wish for three more wishes on your third wish."

"I know, I know, all talk and no customer service." Argued King Alloicious.

"Now, your majesty. I try to give the best customer service I can give." Explained Seán. "I tried to offer you a fifty percent discount for those extra wishes, to which you refused."

"You didn't even accept my coupons!" cried King Alloicious waving a small book of coupons.

"We weren't a participating business for your silly little scalped coupons!" debated Seán.

In trying to explain to the kingdom what had happened, it lead to everyone arguing with each other. Everyone was at each other's throats due to the Ministry's instilled confusion amongst the people. On the inside Richard was becoming more and more panicked.

"Enough!" he shouted loudly. Everyone in the kingdom became silent. "I stole the ball of wisdom, because I wanted to learn more about humans, because I was afraid to actually meet humans. However, Crystal changed that when she found me... Then you were all kidnapped by the Ministry, to which we saved you all with carrot cake and bagpipes. Now, we've come to return the ball of wisdom." The people of the kingdom all began to whisper to each other quietly.

"I'm sorry for causing all this trouble." Sighed Richard. "Kelly, please get off my back."

"I didn't even say anything to you!" Kelly protested.

"No. Kelly, you're on my back. I would like you to get off so I can fly away and be alone." Explained Richard.

"Oh, my apologies."

Kelly jumped off of Richard's back, landing next to Crystal. Richard looked at Crystal for a moment, feeling ashamed, then flew away. As he flew away, Crystal felt a compassion for Richard. Her mind began to race as she concocted a plan to help her now good friend Richard. This, however, was unbeknownst to him as he roamed the courtyard of his castle, quietly polishing his collection of shiny objects. He didn't know why, but he felt bad for what he said, as he polished replaying the event over in his head.

"Hey." A voice greeted.

In surprise Richard turned his head to see Crystal, standing behind him alone. She stood grinning awkwardly and gave a faint wave.

"Hi." Richard also smiled awkwardly.

"That was quite a speech back there." Stated Crystal.

Richard then hung his head low in shame.

"I'm sorry..." he sighed. "I don't know what came over me... I guess I wasn't one hundred percent ready to integrate socially... So when I saw everyone arguing, I kind of lost it."

"It happens." Crystal said as she held Richard's scaly paw. Her hands were soft and warm. He smiled faintly to himself.

"You know the Ministry, tried to trick me too."

"Did they?" asked Crystal.

"Yes. One of their demons changed themselves to look almost exactly like you." Explained Richard. "The fake version of you tried to play head games with me, by saying terrible things and making it look like it was coming from you."

"I see." Nodded Crystal.

"However, I knew it wasn't you." Richard then smiled at Crystal. "I know in my heart that you would never say those kinds of things, because, you're a good person and an even better friend."

"You're not too bad yourself there dragon." Crystal lightly punched him as a gesture of friendship.

"So, I'm curious, why are you here?" inquired Richard.

"Well... we all talked to King Alloicious." Explained Crystal. "He felt that the ball of wisdom should be better protected, seeing as how you liked it so much, even to go so far as steal it." She chuckled lightly. "Not to mention you wanted to learn more about us humans. So, King Alloicious has offered you a job guarding the ball of wisdom in the kingdom."

Richard was almost in disbelief as he pinched himself lightly to make sure he wasn't in a dream. He did however, have a few questions.

"Are living quarters included?" he asked.

"Yes." Replied Crystal.

"Meals?"

"Yes."

"Dental?"

"Yes."

"Vacation days?"

"Yes."

"Severance pay?"

"Yes."

"Stock options?"

"That one you're going to have to talk with King Alloicious on your own." Chuckled Crystal.

"I'll take the job." Nodded Richard proudly.

He was overjoyed with his new job. He danced around the courtyard happy as ever. Then Richard looked at all of his shiny, gleaming possessions. Also remembering all of his books and furnishings in his castle.

"There's just one problem..." he frowned. "I have all this stuff... I'll never be able to move to the kingdom, or at least not for many, many months."

"We thought of that." Grinned Crystal. "Follow me." She gestured.

Following Crystal's lead, Richard ventured out of his castle courtyard. In the clearing where he and Crystal had once done battle and became friends were the people of the kingdom. Leading the crowd were Mary Ann and Seán, with Mary Ann awkwardly trying to avoid him, Margaret, and Joan, holding a freshly baked batch of carrot cake, Michael and his band dressed in their clan tartaned kilts, and Kelly well, she was playing Cleavers and Trolls with Anthony, Hugh, and Wyllo. Richard was now slightly emotional and had many questions.

"How? Why?"

"I believe I can explain that." Disclosed Seán. "You see, as it turns out, King Alloicious's coupons were redeemable for three free wishes after all. So, we brought everyone here voluntarily to help you move."

"Wait a minute!" shouted Fairy Lewis from the crowd. "You said we were getting paid for this!"

"Well, almost everyone came here on a voluntary basis..." shrugged Seán.

Richard could feel a slight lump in his throat, as he looked at the crowd ready to help him move and most importantly the people that he had met and become friends with were also there to support him.

"I don't know what to say." He said.

Then from out of the crowd, Mr. Sinclair and Manuel presented themselves.

"Perhaps we can help you know what to say." He stated in his upper-class British accent. "Manuel and I are your executive object organization movers, and you can say to us what you would like moved to your new home. Isn't that right Manuel?"

"Que?"

"Oh dear, not this again." Mr. Sinclair fumed, while putting his hand on his forehead to keep himself calm.

"Why, thank you." Nodded Richard. "Whatever isn't nailed to the floor, take it away."

"Right! You can count on us." Beamed Mr. Sinclair.

"Que?" asked Manuel.

"I wasn't talking to you..."

"Que?"

"Just get in the castle!" He shouted and pointed angrily.

As Manuel walked past Crystal, they both exchanged a wink.

"What- what was that?" Mr. Sinclair asked Crystal. "You two just shared a wink."

"Que?" she replied giggling.

"Simply infuriating!" Shouted Mr. Sinclair as he stormed off into the castle.

"Oh dear... I'm never going to find any of my stuff again." Frowned Richard.

"Don't worry, they're..." Crystal paused for moment as they heard Mr. Sinclair shouting numerous insults. "Fairly capable at what they do."

"Well then." Smiled Richard happily, then turned his gaze to the crowd. "Let's get to work everyone!"

With that the crowd rushed into the castle. They worked together like ants, as they packed and carried whatever they could out of Richard's castle. While this was a somewhat exhausting job, the people managed to sing and dance happily as they worked. You may insert a musical number here. Crystal had also diligently put herself in charge of packing Richard's mass library of books. The day was almost over as the last few pieces of furniture were packed off to the kingdom. Meanwhile Crystal and Richard sat in the now empty courtyard sharing some carrot cake.

"You know..." Richard said after swallowing his first bite. "Your grandma does make a pretty good carrot cake."

"Your damn right I do!" shouted Margaret proudly, as she came outside with Joan, Mary Ann, and Seán.

"Everything has been brought to Richard's new home." Stated Joan. "Crystal, we're going to head home with everyone else now."

"Would it be all right if I stayed with Richard then came home with him?" asked Crystal.

Richard clearly smiled, happy at the thought. Joan seeing his smile, sighed and thought for a moment.

"I suppose..." she agreed reluctantly.

"Thank you, mom." Smiled Crystal.

"Just be back in time for supper." Joan said sternly.

"Yes, mom."

"Speaking of supper." Joan then turned to Seán. "Seán, would you like to join us?"

"I would love to, but Mary Ann and I must re-build the Closet of Knowledge." Explained Seán.

"Just the two of us?" giggled Mary Ann excitedly, at the prospect of being alone with Seán.

Everyone looked at Mary Ann curiously, as a reaction from her awkward behaviour.

"No." replied Seán completely oblivious as to how Mary Ann felt about him. "Michael will be there too."

"Oh..." sighed Mary Ann feeling embarrassed.

"All right Crystal, we're going to head home now." Stated Joan. "You two behave." She threatened sarcastically by wagging her finger in front of them.

Crystal and Richard watched from the courtyard as everyone waved goodbye to them and magically disappeared to where they needed to be. It was now just Richard and Crystal sitting silently atop the castle wall, watching the sun set. Crystal leaned her head down laying on Richard, however he awkwardly pulled himself away.

"You know Richard the sun is setting." Stated Crystal. "Do you know what that means?"

"Yes." Smiled Richard. "We're the heroes of the adventure, and the adventure is now coming to an end after being through so much, thus completing the hero's journey."

"Well I was going to say that the sun set means that it's getting late, and we should probably get going or my mom will kill us, but what you said, that too."

Richard laughed. "Get on Crystal, let's go home."

I'm not going to cry, I'm not going to cry, I'm not going to cry... Deep breath in, 1, 2, 3, 4, 5... and exhale. As our heroes flew back to the kingdom, the setting sun bathed the land in a magical orange colour. At the pub back in Scotland, Michael, Seán, and Mary Ann were currently trying to make a new Closet of Knowledge.

"Let me see here, slot A goes into slot B..."

"Ack, Seán, we've been at this for five hours." complained Michael.

"I'm telling you two, this is the last time we get a Closet of Knowledge out of a cereal box." decreed Mary Ann.

So, as our adventure finally comes to a close, I guess you could say that everyone lived happily-

"No."

Come on Crystal, I must end the story some way.

"You can end it any way you want, just not that way. It's way too cliché."

All right fine, have it your way, but honestly that's all I had to end this story.

"That's all right; I've got a wiser way. You might say that, in this story we had a real ball."

The End

(Well... Not exactly.)

Acknowledgments

They say in life,

"Everything happens for a reason."

In my opinion, acknowledgements are basically one big thank you for "Everything" that happened for the reasons of writing a book. So here 1 am sitting at my desk, thinking of all the people that Crystal and 1 want to thank. There's honestly a fair bit of people, those who encouraged us, those who gave us money to do this, and even those who tried to knock us down. Of course, in this we're going to focus more on those who gave their unending support. First Crystal's parents and my parents... Personally, 1 think all four of you are nuts. Reason being, we cause literal terror when we're toddlers, and you put up with us. However, it doesn't end there. We then become teenagers, you try to set dating rules for us like,

"We're not allowed to date until we're 16"

But we break those rules anyways, and now we have a book... it was an accident... we didn't think it would happen... we thought if it was the first time for a couple, we would get a trial run... are we ready for such a responsibility? Not to mention instead of putting a stop to this bad behaviour, you encouraged it, and paid for it (Thanks dad, we owe you). Anyways, thank you from the bottom of our hearts and we can't wait to move out of the house when we're 18. Speaking of family, there's a certain someone to blame… I mean thank for all of this, because it's quite possible that none of this would have happened if it hadn't have been for you. Thank you, Marnie, for introducing me to the hazel eyed, book nerd, enigma of a girl that is your grand daughter Crystal. You said to me one day that putting Crystal and I together was the best thing you ever did. Hey, Crystal and I, we're not arguing with you on that one.

Friends, the 2nd most important thing to have in life next to family, and no I'm not talking about the TV show. Jacob, thank you for donating money to the GoFundMe that I set up to pay for The Ball of Wisdom to be self-published. You gave a lot more than just 25 dollars. You gave me hope and encouragement that this was something I could accomplish. Kelly, both Crystal and I want to thank you, because you let us put you in the book. After talking with you for a total of one email (which is all I need), Crystal is very lucky to have such a caring, supportive friend like you by her side.

I also want to thank youtuber Alex Clark, for taking the time out of his busy schedule to record some voice over lines for the Ball of Wisdom, to help me promote the story. You can check out his channel at ItsAlexClark.

I would like to thank the amazing people at Tellwell self-publishing in Victoria, for helping produce this eccentric, zany little book into something eccentric, zany people randomly find on the store bookshelf.

The bookshelf reminds me of one more person to thank, you, the reader. You pulled this off the bookshelf to read, and that deserves an uncountable amount of thanks from both Crystal and me. The dream is to write a book, make a ton of cash, and appear on Oprah. However for both of us the dream is having you the reader, pick up this book, checking out the back cover to see if it's any good, maybe having a little chuckle and either buying it for your nightstand, or putting it back on the book store shelf, thinking, "Pffft, that's way too much money to pay for a book like this." Thank you.

You are all amazing people, who believed in us when there were times that we couldn't believe in ourselves.

Sincerely,

Ye Writer, Zephram Tino
Ye Illustrator, Crystal Musseau

The Writer And The Illustrator

Gather round everybody for I have a story to tell you.

Long ago, in the far-off Province of British Columbia. In a small village called Langley a boy was born to over age 40 parents on July 15, 2004, he received the name, Zephram. A name that stood for bravery, courage, and warp drive. Two years later February 18, 2006 in another village, some 600 kilometres away called Vernon, a girl was born to under age 20 parents. She received the name of Crystal. Little did anyone realize that the fates had something in mind for these two and that their paths would meet 15 years later.

The boy grew to be a strapping young lad, showing a passion for the literary works of many. Many a day he would spend his time dreamin' of becoming a great writer. Finding himself going to young Author's conferences, being recognized and awarded but alas never published. There isn't any money in being an unpublished author, so soon he found himself working for the Queen as a cook. Which Queen you may ask? The Dairy Queen, in the kingdom of Clearwater.

The girl became a beautiful young flower, passionate about her books, but most passionate about her art, always able to visualize words on a piece of paper and turn it into a visual work of art. Being the eldest child in her family, she sought to protect her younger siblings from any harm. Unfortunately, no suitor in the kingdom of Nova Scotia wanted her hand, but in her defense, she didn't want their hands either.

It was on a fine spring day in 2019, when Zephram and Crystal's paths would finally meet. For you see, while Crystal lived-in far-off lands, her grandmother, Madam Marnie, worked with Zephram for the Queen of Dairy. She approached Zephram, with an offer he could not refuse.

"I will give ye my granddaughter's contact info for which ye can communicate with her, but beware of her mother, who is my daughter. For Crystal's mother is a protective lass when it comes to boys your age, but I will admit that you are different."

When they met, their attraction to each other was almost bewitching. Crystal's mother Jelisa had once said that Zephram had cast a spell on her daughter. Most of the locals would swear this is true, for after Crystal had met Zephram she mysteriously picked up a pencil and dictionary and began to write words and stories. Something which she had never done. One day Crystal had drawn a dragon for Zephram, making the request that he write a story about the drawing. Zephram wrote one part and one part only, but at the end put on a "to be continued". Little did he realize that the fair Crystal hated cliff hangers. Zephram wrote a second part and a second part only. However, there was a "to be continued", just in case. A few months went by, as their relationship began to bloom, darkness and evil came into their lives. Crystal's younger siblings were suddenly snatched away from her mother by a great and powerful force. Relationships were wickedly shattered. However, they would get to see the children every so often, but it would never be the same in Crystal's house without her siblings. For Zephram, it was the loss of his job.

"You are untrustworthy!" his employer proclaimed, yelling in Zephram's face.

With a shattered confidence he left his place of work, wandering aimlessly through the village. He wrote a message to Crystal to tell her what happened. She was compassionate and did her best to help Zephram and take his mind off what was going on. It was that day that Zephram learned the people who truly cared about him will always be there for him. Zephram did return to his place of work, but it was never the same. A joyous place it once was, but a joyous place it is no more. He quit. With darkness in both their lives they sought light in each other, seeking asylum in their own little world known as The Ball of Wisdom. The story got more illustrations, and even more parts. They based their world off the real world. People you read about in this story are based off real people.

So, if you're wondering how you came into possession of this book, the reasons are because of a good grandmother, a bad employer, and a government organization of force with lame names.

"Seán? What the heck are you doing on my laptop?"

Oh Zephram, good to see you lad. You were havin' so much trouble writing the About the Author/Illustrator, so 1 wrote a little something that hopefully you can use.

"This is actually pretty cool."

Thank you.

"We'll use it."

Zephram, Can 1 write the next one?

"We'll see Seán, we'll see."

Zephram Tino

Crystal Musseau

Jim Rimmer &
The Alexander Quill Font

A story within a story.

Picture this, Vancouver, B.C., 1991. A printing press and lithograph type font company wants a 5 minute corporate video so says Gerald Giampa of Giampa Textware. My father, friend of a friend of Gerald Giampa and studying video production at the time, got the job. You can see the corporate video on Youtube here:

https://www.youtube.com/watch?v=46GScrMCvLw&t=3s

Jim Rimmer is the distinguished gentleman in the Mickey Mouse sweatshirt in the video. My father swears that Jim deliberately wore the Disney shirt as a private message Jim wanted to convey. My father is a firm believer in the Termite Terrace "No Session" philosophy and the sweatshirt figures prominently in the video along with a certain aristocratic, well groomed orange Tabby Cat and a camera shy Giampa.

The work with fonts and traditional printing presses that Jim and Gerald accomplished in their lifetime has always fascinated my father. The printing press and its related fonts have a certain distinguished class about them. His corporate video production reflects this. It was this fascination and a remembrance of Gerald that my father recently

Googled his name and learned he had passed away in the early 2000's. A web site has been established in Gerald Giampa's honour. You can find it here:

https://p22.com/lanston/giampa/GiampaIntroduction.html

My father knew that Jim and Gerald and the crew were taking traditional printing press fonts from brass templates and digitizing them for computer use. A painstakingly slow process according to the video. A massive undertaking.

What my father did not know is that Jim Rimmer was also a font creator. He created numerous fonts and I am honoured and proud to be able to use one of Jim Rimmer's distinguished Fonts, **Alexander Quill,** in the text of my book. I found it soft on the eyes while also being representative of Medieval times in which the plot of this book is set.

I pay tribute to these men of printing press class and share with the world the realm of a dying breed.

Thank-you, Jim Rimmer, Canadatype, Richard Kegler, of P22 Type Foundry and a special thanks to my father for having the coolest of connections in this world and for using them to further my career as a writer.

Jim Rimmer Photo by Anna Prior Photography

CPSIA information can be obtained
at www.ICGtesting.com
Printed in the USA
BVHW061955280321
603370BV00002B/4